Toenails, Tonsils, and Tornadoes

Then Tim snapped his fingers. "We'll put the tape recorder in Caroline's room, right by the vent. When she hears Aunt Henrietta snoring, Caroline can turn on the tape."

"Then we'll have to tell Caroline," I said reluctantly. "What if she tattles?"

Tim thought about that. "She can't. If she lets us do it, she'd be in trouble, too. And if she says no, we'll deny the whole thing."

We took the recorder and knocked on Caroline's door. She agreed immediately.

When I looked surprised at how easy it had been to convince her, she shrugged. "She's driving me crazy. This afternoon after school I was watching TV. Aunt Henrietta spent ten minutes telling me about all the chores she had to do when she was my age."

The sound of Aunt Henrietta's voice drifted up the stairs. "I think I'll go to bed," she was telling Mom.

"Here we go," Tim said. "'Operation Get Rid of Aunt Henrietta' is about to begin."

Toenails, Tonsils, and Tornadoes

Bonnie Pryor

illustrated by
HELEN COGANCHERRY

A Beech Tree Paperback Book • New York

The Library of Congress has cataloged the Morrow Junior Books
edition of Toenails, Tonsils, and Tornadoes as follows:
Pryor, Bonnie.
Toenails, tonsils, and tornadoes / Bonnie Pryor ; illustrated by Helen Cogancherry.
p. cm.
Summary: Martin weathers the fourth grade while suffering through the prolonged visit
of a difficult aunt and enduring the trials of a classic "middle child."
ISBN 0-688-14885-9
[1. Family life—Fiction. 2. Aunts—Fiction. 3. Schools—Fiction.]
I. Cogancherry, Helen, ill. II. Title.
PZ7.P94965To 1997 [Fic]—dc20 96-30637 CIP AC

1 3 5 7 9 10 8 6 4 2
First Beech Tree Edition, 1999
ISBN 0-688-16675-X

To my newest grandchild, Sharon,
who doesn't have red hair,
and her father, Rick, because he does

Contents

1

Weird Relatives and Toilet Flushes

DID YOU EVER wonder if you were born into the wrong family? I think about that a lot. It's as if some angel decided to play a practical joke on the day I was born. "See that Snodgrass family down there on earth?" he said to the other angels. "They live in New Albany, Ohio. Everyone in town knows they're special. The dad's a doctor, and in a few years the mom's going to be mayor. They have a sports star son and a brainy daughter. Now baby number three is coming along. Let's put an *ordinary* kid in the family for a change and see what happens. Then later we'll give him a really cute little brother."

Some joke.

When I was little, friends of my parents adopted a baby. For a long time after that, I was sure that I had been adopted, too. One day I finally got enough courage to ask my mom about it. She just pointed to our family picture that's sitting on the coffee table. There we all were, lined up. There was my brother Tim, my sister, Caroline, my little brother Robbie, and me. All of us with our red hair and freckles just like Dad's.

"What do you think?" Mom asked.

"Maybe I just got put in the wrong body," I said.

I know I could never be like my brother Tim. His whole room is about to sink with the weight of all his sports trophies. I'm pretty good at math, but that's nothing compared to Caroline. She's eleven, only a year older than I am. But she is two years ahead of me at school because she's so smart. When I look in the mirror I see a fairly nice face, but of course Robbie, my little brother, is much cuter.

My sister, Caroline, has a theory about it. "If you ordinary, boring people weren't around," she said, "how would anyone know he or she was amazing? Take me, for instance," she added brightly. "Next to you I positively shine."

I have to admit her theory does make sense.

I guess I really don't have much to complain about. I have a new puppy named Sam, and he's finally housebroken, so Mom and Dad let him sleep in my room at night. He's supposed to sleep on the floor, but every morning when I wake up, he's on the bed beside me.

My fourth-grade teacher, Miss Lawson, is the prettiest teacher in the whole school. When I started fourth grade, Jamie was my best friend. He decided that this was our year to be popular, but I got bored hanging around with the cool kids. I ended up with a new best friend named Willie and even a girlfriend named Marcia—although sometimes I wished that I hadn't. So mostly, things were going along pretty well.

Then one Saturday a letter came. I was on the couch, miserable with a sore throat and cold. It was my third cold that winter, and it was only the middle of January.

Dad carried the letter in from the mailbox. He held it between his fingers as if he were holding a piece of moldy bread. "I suppose this is from one of your crazy relatives," he teased as he handed it to Mom. "Henrietta Somebody? The name is pretty smudged."

Mom fingered the envelope. "Henrietta," she repeated. "I do have a cousin Henrietta. But why would she be writing from a post office box in Washington, D.C.?"

Dad got a strange look on his face. "Cousin Henrietta. Is she the one who gave our wedding present to a perfect stranger?"

"No," Mom said. "That was Aunt Abigail. And she didn't mean to give our present away. She got mixed up and went to the wrong wedding."

Caroline looked up from the thousand-piece puzzle she was putting together on the dining room table.

"Your aunt went to the wrong wedding?" she asked. Mom's weird relatives were the subject of many family stories.

"Not on purpose," Mom said, a little defensively. "She hadn't seen me for years, and the other wedding was only a block away."

"So which one is Cousin Henrietta?" Dad asked. "I can't seem to place her. Where does she live?"

Mom was a long time answering. "Nowhere, really."

Tim tore his eyes away from the basketball game he was watching on television. "Your cousin is a bag lady?" he screeched. Actually it didn't start out as a screech. Tim's voice has been doing strange things lately.

"Of course not," Mom said. "Most of the time she stays with Aunt Abigail. But they don't always get along. So every now and then Cousin Henrietta visits people. The last I heard, she was visiting my brother John."

Dad had a wild look in his eye. "Just how long has she been visiting John?"

"About six months," Mom mumbled.

"Read the letter," Dad ordered. He looked grim.

Mom meekly tore open the envelope. We all sort of held our breath and stared at her as she read.

"Well?" Dad asked after several minutes.

"She's on her way," Mom said in a small voice. It was quiet for a minute.

4

"On her way *now*?" asked Dad.

"There is one thing, though," Mom said. A smile twitched in the corners of her mouth. "It's not my cousin Henrietta. It's your aunt Henrietta."

Dad grabbed the letter and stared at it. "I haven't seen Aunt Henrietta since I was about twelve years old. I don't remember very much about her. She's my father's sister. She works for an international relief organization of some sort. Come to think of it, it *was* based in Washington. I know she was teaching school in India. Before that, she lived in South America. I can't imagine why she would be coming for a visit after all these years."

"She says in the letter that she has been away so long that she wants to get reacquainted with her family. I think it's a good idea," Mom said in her no-nonsense mayor voice. "The children should know more of their relatives."

"I suppose she's a real prim and proper old lady," Tim said. He sighed. "We will have to drink tea and look at slide shows."

"Hey, wait a minute," Caroline said, examining the letter. "Why is her name Jones instead of Snodgrass, like ours?"

"That was her husband's name," Dad answered. "He died a long time ago."

"How long is she going to stay?" I asked.

Mom consulted the letter. "She doesn't say."

"Where is she going to sleep?" Caroline asked.

Mom looked thoughtful. "That is going to be a problem." She frowned. "Martin, you could sleep in Tim's room, since he has the extra bunk bed. And Aunt Henrietta can sleep in your room."

I groaned. In the first place, there was hardly enough space in Tim's room for Tim and all his trophies. In the second place, after a night in a room with Tim's sneakers I might never wake up again.

Just then Robbie came toddling into the room with his pants down around his ankles. "I pooped," he said proudly. "Come see, Martin."

"I'll go," Mom said. Robbie just started going to the bathroom by himself. But someone always has to go admire it and tell him what a good boy he is.

Robbie stuck out his lower lip. "Want Martin to see," he said.

With a sigh, I followed him down the hall to the downstairs bathroom and looked in the toilet. "Wow, that's great," I said automatically. "You're a big boy," I added as I reached for the handle.

"Robbie flush," he yelled. He pushed the handle just as I noticed something bright green swirling around in the water.

"Dad!" I shouted. But it was too late. Robbie's favorite green car disappeared down the hole.

2

Dog Barks
and Smelly Sneakers

THE PLUMBERS DIDN'T get to our house until Sunday morning. Aunt Henrietta arrived just as they were leaving. Dad was waving his checkbook around in the air. "Two hundred and fifty dollars! The next time someone messes up the plumbing, please don't do it on the weekend. That has got to be the most expensive flush in the history of mankind."

Robbie stuck out his lip. "Robbie likes to flush."

"Of course you do," boomed a voice from the door.

I stared in amazement. The speaker was at least six feet tall. Her hair was gray, with just enough red left to identify her as a Snodgrass. It was piled up on her head, making her look even taller. Under all that hair was a nice face with a rather large nose. Bony

8

elbows poked out from under the rolled-up sleeves of an old sweatshirt. Bright red plaid pants and sturdy brown shoes covering the largest feet I had ever seen completed the picture.

There was a moment of awkward silence. Everyone sort of froze in place, staring at one another. "Weren't you expecting me?" the weird-looking woman finally said.

"Aunt Henrietta," Dad exclaimed in a strangled voice. "It's so good to see you."

"And there's a lot of her to see," Tim mumbled from behind me.

Aunt Henrietta waved at the taxi driver. He started unloading the taxi and carrying an amazing assortment of suitcases, boxes, and bags into the house. Dad's face looked a little more glum with each piece of luggage.

"This is an awful lot of luggage for a short visit," he whispered to Mom while Aunt Henrietta paid the taxi driver.

Aunt Henrietta didn't seem to notice Dad's concern. She wrapped her long arms around him in a big hug. When he introduced Mom, Aunt Henrietta hugged her, too.

"These are our children," Mom said, and she introduced us one by one. Each of us in turn was smothered in a huge bear hug. When it was Robbie's turn, he barked.

Mom looked embarrassed. "Sometimes Robbie likes to pretend he's a dog."

Aunt Henrietta bent down to Robbie. "Woof, woof," she said solemnly.

"Woof," Robbie replied. He was obviously pleased to find someone who spoke his language.

Suddenly Sam woke up from his nap and discovered there was someone in the house. Sam is not the world's greatest watchdog, obviously. He bounded into the room and added his "Yip yip" to the chorus of barks.

Aunt Henrietta pulled a huge men's handkerchief from her pocket and sneezed. "A-choo. A-choo." She smiled apologetically. "Sorry. I guess I should have warned you I was allergic to dogs."

"Martin, take Sam out to the garage," Mom said.

"But he'll be lonesome," I protested.

"He'll be fine," said Dad with a look that told me I'd better not say any more.

I picked up Sam and stalked out to the garage. Behind me I heard Mom clear her throat. "Why don't I introduce you to Mrs. Albright," she said cheerfully. "She's our housekeeper." Aunt Henrietta followed Mom to the kitchen. Dad picked up four suitcases and grimly headed for my bedroom.

I found an old piece of rug for Sam and made a bed for him near the back door. When I sat down on it, Sam whined softly and put his head on my knee.

"It's not fair, is it, Sam? You were here first. I already have to give her my room, and now this. I hope she doesn't stay very long."

Sam just looked at me with mournful eyes. When I went back in the house, the grown-ups were talking around the kitchen table.

"Robbie likes Dog Lady," Robbie said. He trailed past me into the kitchen.

I found Tim and Caroline in the living room. Caroline rolled her eyes. "Weird!" she said. "I wonder what Mrs. Albright will think about her?"

Everyone in the family loves Mrs. Albright. She's more like an extra grandma than a house-keeper. She and Mr. DeWitt, our next-door neighbor, go to concerts and movies together. Right now they are really good friends. But Mrs. Albright told me if they ever do get married, we'll still be like her own family.

"Maybe Aunt Henrietta is barking at her," Tim said.

We listened, but the conversation coming from the kitchen seemed to be friendly.

Dad left to visit patients in the hospital, and Mom came back into the living room. "They're chatting like old friends," she said. "This is a good time to change the beds around. And we will have to vacuum thoroughly to make sure we get all the dog hair out of Martin's bedroom."

Mom rolled the vacuum into my room and started cleaning everything in sight.

"Mom's getting all your cooties out of there," Caroline said with a smirk.

I ignored her as I carried my things to Tim's room and tried to find a place for my clothes in his closet.

"You can sleep in the top bunk," Tim said.

"I don't like the top," I said. "What if I fall out?"

"Tough," Tim said cheerfully. "It's my room."

Tim plopped down on the bottom bunk, his sneakers only a few feet from my nose. Suddenly I felt better. At least up on the top bunk I would be that much farther away from Tim's smelly feet.

Aunt Henrietta was busy unpacking when I passed by my bedroom door. Mom had already cleared off my dresser and shelves. My fuzzy bedspread had been replaced with a quilt, and a stack of old-lady clothes was on my bed. The room had turned into her room. It was as though it had never been mine.

"Nice room," she said. "Yours?"

"It was," I said grimly. "I have to sleep in Tim's room while you're here."

Aunt Henrietta didn't seem to notice how unhappy I was. "I appreciate it," she said. She stuffed an empty suitcase in the closet. "Sorry about the dog. Although I have to admit that I never understood why people want to have animals in the house. Messy creatures. Always drooling and dropping hairs about."

"Sam is a great dog," I shouted. "He never drools." I stomped downstairs and threw myself in a living room chair.

"You look like a thunderstorm about to happen," said Mrs. Albright. She arranged some magazines on the coffee table she had just dusted. "What's the trouble?"

"I hate her," I blurted out. "First she takes my room and messes it all up. And I'll bet she just pretended to sneeze to get rid of Sam. She thinks dogs don't belong in the house."

"I'm sure she wouldn't have done that," Mrs. Albright said. "I don't think Sam will mind being in the garage that much if you take him out for walks. I have an old laundry basket. If we put an old blanket in it, I think he will be pretty comfortable." She patted my arm. "It's only for a few days."

Mrs. Albright helped me make up the bed for Sam. I carried his food and water dishes to the garage. When we went back inside, Aunt Henrietta had just come downstairs. "Like to run?" she asked.

"Run?" I echoed.

She ran a few steps in place to demonstrate. "You know, run."

"I'm not very athletic," I said, not looking at her.

Aunt Henrietta snorted. "You don't have to be athletic to run. I run every day. It's good for your heart. Young people today don't get enough exercise." As she spoke, she pulled on a beat-up pair of running shoes. "We can take it easy today. Just a few warm-ups and a short run. We won't go far."

"No thanks," I answered crossly. "I'm just getting over a cold."

Dad walked in just in time to hear the conversation. "I think you are well enough for a little run, Martin. Aunt Henrietta doesn't know her way around the neighborhood. We wouldn't want her to get lost on her first day."

I tried to think of another excuse. "I don't have any running shoes."

Aunt Henrietta frowned thoughtfully at my shoes. "Those will do for now. I'll talk to your mother about getting some proper ones."

Miserably I put on my jacket. The last thing I wanted to do was go running, and certainly not with an old woman I didn't even like.

Then Caroline came downstairs. "Robbie and I are going running," Aunt Henrietta informed her.

"I'm Martin," I protested. If she was going to kill me with embarrassment, she could at least remember my name.

"Of course you are," said Aunt Henrietta.

Caroline's grin went nearly from ear to ear. "I'll bet you have a wonderful time," she said. "All that fresh air and exercise."

"Why don't you join us, too," Aunt Henrietta said.

"Yeah, Caroline," I said. "Then you can get some of that good fresh air and exercise yourself."

"I would really love to," Caroline said, almost convincingly. "But unfortunately I am going to my friend's house to practice for the spelling bee. I was last year's state champion."

"You got that from your great-grandpa Snodgrass," Aunt Henrietta said. "He won the state championship in 1927. He would have won for the whole country, but he got tripped up by the word *logistically*."

"L-o-g-i-s-t-i-c-a-l-y," Caroline said.

"Nope. Same mistake your great-grandfather made. There are two *l*'s."

Caroline's face looked dark as she hurried off to look it up in the dictionary. "Don't bother," Aunt Henrietta called cheerfully after her. "I'm pretty good at spelling myself."

She reached for the door. "Ready?" she asked.

"I wanna go, too." My little brother left the pile of cars he'd been racing across the dining room floor.

"Not this time, Martin," Aunt Henrietta said.

"I'm Robbie," Robbie shouted.

Aunt Henrietta patted his cheek as we went outside. "Of course you are."

3

Do Families Grow
on Trees?

ON WEDNESDAY, MISS Lawson passed out some papers. "We've been studying United States history," she said. "Families have histories, too. As a matter of fact, the histories of all our families make up the history of our country. The founders of our country were somebody's great-great-grandfathers." She stopped and stared at Willie. He was leaning back in his chair, whistling the song "Dixie."

"Willie, why are you whistling when I am talking?" she asked.

Willie sat up straight. "I was listening," he protested. "But I thought maybe some of our ancestors might have come from the South."

"This is just a paper, Willie. It doesn't need sound

effects." Miss Lawson's pretty face looked stern.

Willie shrugged. "Sorry, but I'll bet it would be more fun with music."

Miss Lawson sighed, but I thought I saw her lips twitch as though she were fighting a smile. I looked at the sheet she had handed me. It was labeled "My Family Tree" and showed a tree with spaces to write in names.

"One of my ancestors came over on the *Mayflower*," Marcia said.

"Too bad," Lester said loudly. "I heard it was a pretty nice country until then."

Miss Lawson frowned. "I'm sure that everyone has some good *and* some not so good characters in their family tree. Sometimes learning about our families can help us understand ourselves. For instance, Jason is a very good artist. It may be that somewhere in his family tree is an ancestor who was very artistic."

"My mom and dad came to America just before I was born," Brianne said shyly. "All my ancestors come from Italy." Brianne was the new girl. Her hair was so curly that it bounced when she moved her head. She always smelled like vanilla. "My parents miss Italy," she continued. "All my grandparents live there. But I miss California. We lived right near the ocean, and it was almost always warm."

"Is Brianne an Italian name?" Marcia asked.

"No, my parents wanted me to have an American

name," Brianne answered. "The lady who lived next door to us in California helped my parents a lot when they came to this country. Her name was Brianne."

"We are going to be studying the states for the next few months," Miss Lawson said. "Why don't you plan to tell us about California?"

"Do we have to turn these family tree papers in?" Willie interrupted.

"No, you don't have to turn these in," Miss Lawson said. "I just thought it might be fun for you to see how much information about your family you can find out. If there's anything interesting you want to share, let me know."

"I'll bet I have all kinds of interesting ancestors," Marcia said smugly.

"I'll bet you have all kinds of ugly ancestors," Lester mumbled.

"Miss Lawson, Lester is making fun of me again," Marcia complained.

"That's enough," Miss Lawson said tiredly. She started our math lesson, so I tucked my family tree paper in my notebook and forgot about it until after school.

At lunchtime I hobbled to the cafeteria. I walked past Jamie and his friends Steve and Lester and sat down by myself. Willie Smith slid his tray on the table.

At first, I hadn't liked Willie very much. He'd been

left back a year at school, and he always seemed to be causing trouble. But Willie turned out to be a great friend. We both joined the community Youth Theater, and Willie got the lead role in a musical play based on *The Adventures of Tom Sawyer*.

"What's wrong with you?" Willie asked as I groaned. Every muscle in my body ached.

"I had to run about ten miles last night," I said. "Trying to catch up to Aunt Henrietta."

Willie's mouth froze just as he was about to bite into a peanut butter sandwich. "Your aunt was trying to run away?"

"Exercise running," I explained, laughing at his confused expression. "She said we only ran about a mile." I rubbed my sore leg muscles. "But it sure seemed like more."

"Why does she need so much exercise?" he asked.

I shook my head. "Because she's crazy."

"You'd better put her in your family tree. Then your tree will have a crazy branch. Like a crazy bone. Get it?" Willie hooted at his own joke.

"Are you ready for tonight?" I asked him, changing the subject. Tonight was the first dress rehearsal for *The Adventures of Tom Sawyer*. Then we were having another run-through tomorrow night, which was Thursday, and then three performances over the weekend. Suddenly it was all happening very fast.

"I'm pretty nervous," he admitted.

I grinned at him. "I would be, too, if I had to kiss Caroline."

Caroline, of course, had the star part of Tom's girl-friend, Becky Thatcher.

Willie shuddered. "I don't want to even think about it."

When we went outside to the playground, Marcia followed. Her round glasses make her look cute, like an owl, but she could be a real pain. "How's Sam doing?" she asked. Marcia had given me Sam when her dog had puppies.

"He was doing great," I said. "Now my aunt is staying with us, and he has to stay in the garage."

Marcia looked sympathetic, but she shrugged. "My mom won't let our dog in the house either."

She was starting to say something else when I noticed Brianne standing nearby. A few flakes of snow drifted down.

"Did you have snow in California?" I asked.

Brianne pulled her coat around tighter. "Not where I lived. Once it snowed when we went to the mountains."

"You'll see lots of it here," I told her.

"I can hardly wait to make a snowman," she said.

"This snow is too dry," I said. I stuck out my tongue and caught a flake. "You have to have just the right kind of snow to make a snowman. I'll show you how when we get a good snow."

Willie came over and sniffed loudly. "You smell like cookies," he announced. A lot of the girls liked Willie, with his curly black hair and blue eyes.

Brianne giggled. "It's my sister's new perfume. It's called Tropical Vanilla." She held out her arm for us to smell. "Do you like it?"

Some of the girls called to Brianne and she ran to join them. Willie and I walked across the playground. Marcia didn't follow us. I looked back and saw her standing by the swings. She did not look happy.

Willie grinned at me. "Looks like your girlfriend is jealous."

"I wish I had a magic wand," I grumbled. "I'd make Aunt Henrietta and Marcia both disappear."

Our neighbor Mr. DeWitt was sitting on his front porch when I got home after school. I let Sam out of the garage, and he bounded around the yard while I talked to Mr. DeWitt.

"Sam probably thinks no one loves him anymore," I said glumly.

"How about my keeping Sam until your aunt leaves?" Mr. DeWitt suggested. "Daffy and I would love the company."

Mr. DeWitt's yellow cat was sitting on the windowsill washing her face with her paws.

"What if Sam forgets me?" I said.

"How could he forget you? You can come over and

21

see him every day. And you can still take him for walks. You might even bring something of yours he can chew on to remind him of you."

I thought for a minute. "There's an old pair of slippers in my closet."

"Why don't you give them to Sam?" he asked.

"Thanks, Mr. DeWitt. That's a good idea." I ran inside and found the slippers and an old shirt. I put them in Sam's bed and carried them all to Mr. DeWitt's house. Daffy arched her back with alarm, but Sam settled right down in his basket, chewing happily.

"Dinner smells good," I said when I walked in the kitchen. We were having an early dinner because of the rehearsal. Mrs. Albright was fixing spaghetti, my favorite. Her sauce is really special.

"I hope it tastes all right," Mrs. Albright said. "I couldn't put any onions in it. Your aunt says they give her indigestion."

"I wish she would leave," I grumbled. "Next I suppose we'll have to eat prunes for breakfast."

Mrs. Albright patted my shoulder. "Give her a chance. She's really a pretty nice lady."

I sighed. "Mom says she's spent her life serving other people and she deserves being treated specially for a while. I suppose that's true. But why did she have to pick us?"

"That spaghetti smells delicious," Aunt Henrietta

said as she came in the kitchen. I gave her a guilty look, wondering if she had heard me, but she just smiled and sat down at the table.

I have to admit that even without onions, the spaghetti was delicious. Caroline only put a few strands on her plate. She pushed them around, not eating.

"There are children in some of the schools where I've taught who would be awfully glad to have some of this spaghetti," Aunt Henrietta remarked.

"I'm not very hungry," Caroline said.

"Are you feeling all right?" Mom asked.

"She's probably on a diet," Tim said gleefully. "She is looking kind of chubby lately."

"That is not a very nice way to talk about your sister," Aunt Henrietta said.

I gritted my teeth. It was true, but what right did she have to say it?

"I was only teasing," Tim mumbled.

"Maybe she's nervous about the rehearsal," I said.

"Will you all quit talking about me as though I wasn't sitting right here?" Caroline shouted. "I am just not hungry." She glared at Tim. "I may be chubby, but at least you can't smell me coming a mile away." Then she turned her glare on me. "And I am not nervous. I know my lines perfectly. I just don't feel like eating."

"I know my lines, too," I said. "And I'm still nervous."

"You only had a few lines to learn," Caroline said in a sour voice.

"I could have learned more. I even know your part—including the songs. I've had to listen to you practicing so much." I sang a few bars to show her.

"Your great-uncle John used to say that every part in a play is important," Aunt Henrietta said.

Robbie rattled on his high-chair tray. "All done," he said.

"Who was Great-Uncle John?" Tim asked.

"He was my grandfather's brother. He traveled all around the West doing Shakespeare's plays. He was quite famous in his day."

"Hey, I could put him in the family tree," I exclaimed. I explained about the paper Miss Lawson had given us.

"All done," Robbie repeated.

"Just a minute, Robbie," Mom said absently. "I can help you with my side of the family, Martin. I'm sure Aunt Henrietta could help you, too. She knows everything about the Snodgrasses."

"These children should know more about their ancestors," Aunt Henrietta said. She snapped her bony fingers. "We should have a family reunion. They'll hear a lot of family history there."

I thought Dad would turn down that idea immediately, but he seemed to be considering it. "It has been a long time since we've all gotten together," he said.

"All done." Robbie banged on his tray with his spoon, but everyone was busy talking.

"My family had a reunion about a year ago," Mom said. "I was so busy with the garbagemen's strike that we couldn't go. I think it would be good for the children to meet more of their family."

"Exactly how many people are we talking about?" Caroline asked.

Aunt Henrietta did some rapid mental math. "We would have to make a list, of course, but I would say fifty to one hundred."

"What do you do at a family reunion?" I asked.

"All *done,*" Robbie said.

"Talk mostly," Dad answered. "Get to know people in your family you didn't even know existed."

"Sounds boring to me," Tim said.

"If we wait until the weather gets warmer, we could have it right here. Maybe like a picnic," Mom said.

"That would be a lot of work," Dad said.

"Not if everyone helped," Mom said. "Tim, you could help organize some activities."

Robbie banged his plate on his tray. "ALL DONE!" he roared.

"My goodness," Mom said. "Why is Robbie so excited?"

I got up and unfastened the tray to release him. The grown-ups hardly noticed, they were so busy finalizing the reunion idea. Tim, Caroline, and I went outside on the porch. Robbie tagged along behind us. I went next door to get Sam and brought him back to our yard. I tossed a ball for him to fetch while we talked.

"I don't know about this idea," Caroline said. Her voice was sounding really scratchy. "Probably some of them will stay at the house. We'll end up sleeping on the floor."

"Aunt Jane and Uncle Dave are pretty nice," Tim said. "We haven't seen them for a while."

"I'll bet Grandma and Grandpa would come from Florida," I said.

"What if there are a bunch of weird relatives like Aunt Henrietta that we don't know?" Caroline asked.

I pointed to Tim's shoes. "If there is anyone we don't like, we can just put a pair of Tim's sneakers in their room. Believe me, the relatives will be gone the next morning."

4

The Great Paint Disaster

MOM HAD A city council meeting after dinner. Some people in town thought that the intersection near the new shopping center was dangerous. They were going to present a petition to have a traffic light installed.

Mrs. Albright had taken Robbie for a walk with Mr. DeWitt and Sam. Dad was going to drop Caroline and me off for our rehearsal on his way to the hospital. That left Tim as the only one at home to go running with Aunt Henrietta.

"Why does she run so much anyway?" Tim grumbled.

"I thought you knew," Dad said. "Aunt Henrietta wants to run in the Boston Marathon."

Tim laughed. "That's ridiculous. She must be sixty

years old. She doesn't have a chance of winning."

"Aunt Henrietta has already qualified. But I don't think she cares about winning," Dad said. "It's just something she always wanted to do. Simply to finish would be great."

"I don't understand," I said. "What is the Boston Marathon?"

"Don't you know anything?" Caroline said, shaking her head. "It's a big race held every year in Boston. Thousands of people run in it, but a lot of them don't make it. It is over twenty-six miles long. It's one of the hardest marathons because of the hills at the end."

"That's stupid," I exclaimed. "Why would anyone want to run that far? Especially an old lady like her."

"I don't think you had better let Aunt Henrietta hear you call her an 'old lady,' " Dad said. "Actually, Aunt Henrietta has competed in several big races all over the world. She has won some trophies, too. But this is the first chance she's had to run in the Boston Marathon. I'd like you kids to help her train. It's good exercise for you." He gave Tim a playful poke. "Running is good training for sports."

"What if somebody sees me?" Tim complained.

"He means, what if any girls see him," Caroline said.

"It's not just the running," Tim grumbled. "Aunt

Henrietta is a real pain. Yesterday Mary Ann Masters called. Aunt Henrietta told her I couldn't come to the phone because I was in the bathroom."

Dad looked puzzled. "Where were you?"

"I was in the bathroom," Tim explained. "But you don't tell that to the prettiest girl in the seventh grade."

"Ah." Dad nodded wisely. "Well, perhaps Aunt Henrietta didn't realize she was talking to the prettiest girl in the seventh grade."

"She really *is* a pain," Caroline agreed. "Every time we talk about something we've done, she knows some kid halfway around the world who did the same thing."

"Only better," Tim mumbled.

Dad turned to me. "I suppose you've got something to add?"

"I miss my own bedroom," I said. "And I hate it that Sam has to stay next door until April." That's when we were having the reunion.

Dad sighed. "I'm sorry you are all so unhappy, but Aunt Henrietta is a guest in our house. The Snodgrass family is always kind to guests. I'm counting on you all to make her feel at home."

Dad dropped Caroline and me off at play practice and headed to the hospital. For months we had been practicing in a church meeting room. Tonight was the first time we were in the theater where the play would be performed. It was a great old building, with a large stage and a huge seating area, that the town used for special events. This was also the first time we'd done the play all the way through with costumes and orchestra.

Marcia Stevens's mother was the director of the play. She looked like a general ordering around an army of parent volunteers. "Everyone go to the green room to get your props and costumes," she shouted over the noise.

We followed the crowd to a huge room in the basement. "This isn't a green room," I whispered to Caroline.

"You are so dumb," Caroline said. "The room where the cast waits during a play is always called a green room."

"Calling a yellow room green sounds pretty dumb to me," I retorted.

Caroline gave me a scornful look. But before she could say more, someone whisked her behind a curtain to help her get changed.

Someone else handed me a pair of bib overalls and showed me where to change.

Marcia was waiting when I was finished. She was wearing a gray wig and old-fashioned glasses, and her clothes were stuffed to make her look plump. She was playing the role of Aunt Polly.

"You look really good," I said.

"Thanks," she said. "You do, too." She paused. "You were talking to Brianne an awful lot today."

"I was just telling her about snow," I said.

Marcia sniffed unhappily. Just then Willie grabbed my arm and pulled me away. "They are putting lipstick on all the boys," he whispered in alarm. "I don't want any of that stuff on me."

Several mothers were rubbing makeup and lipstick on everyone. We stood in line waiting our turn. "I think it is so the people in the audience can see your face," I said.

Willie's grandmother was helping with makeup. She motioned to me. *"Buenas noches,* Martin. *¿Como está usted?"* She rubbed some makeup on my face and dabbed some red color on my lips.

"Grandma is learning Spanish," Willie explained. "She listens to tapes while she is sleeping."

"How can she learn if she is sleeping?" I asked.

Willie shrugged. "I don't know. But it must work. Grandma talks Spanish so much I'm going to have to learn so I can talk to her."

"They're called *subliminal* tapes. Even though you are asleep, a part of your mind hears and remembers," his grandmother explained.

"Why can't we just do that for school?" I asked.

" 'Cause grown-ups like to torture us," Willie said. He looked as if he were being tortured now. His grandmother had finished with me and was smearing makeup on Willie while he squirmed with embarrassment.

"How can girls stand to wear this stuff?" he groaned.

"It will wash right off," his grandmother assured him. "Don't worry, all actors have to put this on."

"I'll bet Arnold Schwarzenegger doesn't," Willie grumbled.

"Oh yes he does," his grandmother answered cheerfully.

Willie still looked doubtful, but he stood still until his grandmother finished.

"You look positively beautiful," I teased.

Willie started to make a fist. Then he grinned. He took his hand and wiped off most of the lipstick. "So do you."

Mrs. Stevens came rushing by. "As soon as you are done here, go see the prop lady," she said.

The prop lady was passing things out in a corner of the yellow "green" room.

When we told her who we were, she checked her list and handed me a straw hat, a fishing pole, and an apple and Willie a can of paint and a brush.

"There's a little bit of real paint in here, so be careful. Just barely dip your brush in. We don't want any dripped on the stage."

My part was of a boy who is tricked by Tom into whitewashing Aunt Polly's fence. I was in the first scene of the play, which was lucky because I was starting to get nervous. My stomach was shaking and my hands were sweaty. I saw Caroline sitting by herself in a corner. She was so pale her freckles stood out like polka dots.

The New Albany High School Orchestra began tuning up, and then it was time for the play to begin. I picked up my pole and tried to look cheerful as I walked out onstage. Willie was there, busy painting the fence and whistling. A long planter filled with flowers sat in front of one end of the fence to make it look more real.

"Too bad you have to paint that old fence. I'm on my way fishing," I said. I reached in my pocket and pulled out the apple.

As Tom, Willie pretended he was having a wonderful time. "This is much more fun than fishing," he said. "Why, I'd choose this to do any day."

"You'd rather paint that fence than go fishing?" I asked.

"Sure would. Why, my aunt Polly picked me special to do this. She wouldn't let just anyone do it."

"Can I try it?" I asked. "I'll give you this apple."

"Well, maybe just for a little bit," Willie said. He handed me the bucket. I dipped my brush very carefully. From where I was standing I had to stretch over the planter to reach the fence. I leaned over, but the can of paint I was holding pulled me out of balance.

I reached for the fence with my other hand, trying desperately to stop myself from falling. Too late I realized my mistake. The fence was only a prop, and of course it couldn't hold me. Slowly the fence tipped over, taking me with it. At the same time the paint can slipped out of my hand and hit the stage with a loud thud. As it rolled away, white paint splattered on me and on Willie, making a big puddle all around the broken fence.

5

Getting Rid of Aunt Henrietta

THE REST OF the dress rehearsal was almost perfect. Willie managed to kiss Caroline without throwing up, and by the time Dad arrived most of the paint had been cleaned away. I still had some sticky spots where paint had dried in my hair.

"You won't believe what Martin did," Caroline tattled to Dad. "He almost managed to wipe out the whole theater production." She told him the whole story while I huddled miserably in the backseat. "Why do I have to be related to him?" Caroline finished with a dramatic wave of her hand. "It's so embarrassing."

"Mrs. Stevens said it could happen to anybody."

Caroline shook her head. "She was just being nice.

No one else in the whole world could be that clumsy. Our second run-through is tomorrow night, and that fence is a disaster!"

"I'm sure Martin feels bad enough without your rubbing it in," Dad said. "I'll call Anne Stevens and see if I can help repair the fence tomorrow," he added. "That should make up for it."

At home, Caroline repeated the story again for Mom and Aunt Henrietta.

"Oh, honey," Mom said to me. "You must have been so embarrassed."

Aunt Henrietta leaned back in her chair. "You don't know it yet, but that was one of the best things that ever happened to you."

"How can you say that?" I sputtered. "It was the worst thing. Everyone laughed at me."

Aunt Henrietta chuckled. "It does sound like it was pretty funny. You would have laughed too if it had happened to someone else. And one of these days you may laugh about it yourself. The Snodgrasses have always loved a good story. Fifty years from now, your children may still be talking about the time Dad almost wiped out the whole production of *Tom Sawyer*. Only by then the story will be that you set off a chain reaction that wiped out the entire set, sent three people to the hospital with broken legs, and spilled a fifty-gallon drum of paint over the entire theater."

I had to smile. "Like when Dad tells us he had to walk five miles to school in snow over his head?" I asked.

"Is that all?" Aunt Henrietta asked. She winked. "One time I had to ride my horse to school. The snow was so deep the poor horse could hardly walk. When I got there, the school was closed. That poor horse of mine was so tired I had to carry him twenty miles back home."

I laughed. "That beats Dad's stories."

"Well, I'm older than your father. My stories have had time to get bigger."

The next morning Willie was waiting for me when I got off the bus. *"Buenas días,"* he said. "That means good morning in Spanish. Grandma is kind of hard of hearing. She plays those tapes so loud I guess I'm learning it, too."

I stared at him. "Say that again."

"Buenas días," Willie repeated.

I waved my hand. "Not that. Tell me about the tapes."

"Grandma listens to her Spanish tapes while she sleeps and in the daytime, too," Willie said patiently. "I guess I'm learning some myself." He shrugged.

I snapped my fingers. "That's it. That's how I can get rid of Aunt Henrietta."

Willie looked blank for a moment. Then he slowly grinned. "You mean that we could make a tape telling her to go home."

"Exactly. If it works for your grandmother, it should work for Aunt Henrietta. I'll just wait until she's asleep and turn it on."

"You had better make the tape at my house. That way no one will find out," Willie said. "Call Mrs. Albright and see if you can come over after school."

Mrs. Albright agreed to pick me up and take me to the rehearsal, so as soon as school was over, Willie and I headed for his house. "Are you sure your grandmother won't mind?" I asked.

Willie's mother had left home when Willie was five. Now he and his father lived with his grandmother not very far from school. At first Willie and his grandmother hadn't gotten along very well. But working together in the play had brought them a lot closer.

"She won't mind," Willie said.

It had snowed the night before, just enough to make a pleasant crunch as we walked. Willie sang some of his favorite commercials, changing the words to make them funny.

"Wait up," Marcia called, running to catch up. She lived close by.

We waited for her. "Are you going to Willie's house?" she asked.

When I nodded, she added, "Why don't you both come home with me? I've got a new sled we could try out on the hill behind my house."

Willie's eyes lit up, and he looked hopefully at me. I thought about that hill. It was perfect for a sled ride. "Maybe for a few minutes," I said.

We stopped to pat Mitzi, Sam's mother, while Marcia took her book bag into the house. Mrs. Stevens made Mitzi stay outside in a little storage shed, but Marcia had made a warm box with rugs and blankets, and there was a little swinging door so Mitzi could go into the yard whenever she wanted to. "We found homes for all of her puppies," Marcia said happily when she returned. She pulled a shiny new sled out of a corner of the shed.

"Wow, that's great," I said. We spent the next half hour taking turns flying down the hill.

"I think my toes are frozen," I finally said.

"I know my fingers are." Willie laughed.

"Mom will make us some hot chocolate," Marcia said as we put the sled away.

We took off our boots and left them outside the door. Mrs. Stevens was pretty fussy about the house. Everything was always perfectly in place. She made us steaming cups of hot chocolate and set them on the kitchen table.

Marcia's family tree paper was displayed on the refrigerator door with a magnet. She noticed me looking at it. "I've almost got everyone filled out," she said. "See, one of my grandfathers was a judge."

"One of my great-uncles went to jail," Willie said cheerfully. "Maybe your grandfather was the judge who sent him there."

Mrs. Stevens's lips set in a disapproving line, but Marcia grinned. "That would be funny, wouldn't it."

"My great-grandfather died in World War II. He got the Medal of Honor for courage," Willie said.

Mrs. Stevens looked relieved. "Maybe you take after him," she said hopefully.

"I don't think so," Willie said. "I haven't noticed anything brave about myself. I think I am just me."

We sipped the drinks while our fingers and toes stopped tingling. "This was fun," I said. At times like these I didn't mind having Marcia for a girlfriend.

I looked at the clock and jumped up in alarm. "Mrs. Albright's picking me up at Willie's house at five," I said.

"You could watch for her from here," Marcia offered.

"I told my grandmother that Martin was coming," Willie fibbed as he pulled his coat on. I thought Marcia looked disappointed that we didn't ask her to come, too, but she didn't say anything. "See you tonight," she said as we left.

Willie's grandmother had fallen asleep watching TV. We tiptoed past her and up a narrow staircase. The house was old and the floors creaked, but I liked Willie's room, which had once been the attic. The ceiling slanted down on each side so that you had to duck your head, but Willie's father had paneled the walls and built shelves and dressers into the small spaces. Willie reached into a drawer and pulled out a tape recorder and a blank tape.

"What should I say?"

He shrugged. "Go home?" he suggested.

I hesitated. Aunt Henrietta had been awfully nice about my making a fool of myself at the dress rehearsal. Still, three more months of her was just too much. Determinedly I spoke into the recorder. "You are terribly homesick, Henrietta. You don't like New Albany. You really want to go home. Home is best."

I repeated it over and over until the tape was full. I switched off the machine.

"That sounded great," Willie said. "This has got to work."

I heard a honk in front of the house. I slipped the tape into my pocket and said good-bye to Willie. I was smiling when I got in the car. "You must have had a good time," Mrs. Albright remarked.

I nodded. I didn't tell her the real reason I was smiling. In no time at all we'd be rid of Aunt Henrietta.

6

Tonsils and Troubles

OUR SECOND DRESS rehearsal was pretty smooth. I managed to get through it without falling or spilling paint on anyone. I came home, dropped my things in Tim's room, and went back downstairs. Aunt Henrietta and Mom were sitting at the dining room table, busily writing invitations to the family reunion.

"I haven't seen Uncle George for years," Mom said. She looked up at me and smiled. "Do you remember Uncle George? He's a geologist. He travels all around the West looking for oil deposits. He visited us a couple of years ago."

I nodded. "He gave me a rock collection."

"One of his daughters is grown-up and married," Aunt Henrietta said thoughtfully. "We don't want to forget her."

I went upstairs to get ready for bed. Tim was sitting on the bottom bunk listening to my tape. He took it out of the player when I walked in the room.

"Hey, that's mine," I said, trying to grab it back.

Tim held it just out of my reach. " 'You want to go home,' " he mocked. He grinned finally and handed it to me. "That is pretty clever. Are you going to hypnotize Aunt Henrietta with it?"

I figured he was as anxious as I was to have Aunt Henrietta leave, so I explained.

"That's a great idea," Tim said thoughtfully. "But how are you going to know when she's asleep?"

"Caroline says she snores. She can hear her through the heating vent. I'm just worried that Aunt Henrietta might wake up and catch me when I turn the tape on."

Tim was silent for a minute. "I just thought of something gross," he said. "When you sneak into Aunt Henrietta's room, what if you see her in her nightgown? Or her underwear?"

"Oh no," I groaned, thinking about the possibility.

Then Tim snapped his fingers. "We'll put the tape recorder in Caroline's room, right by the vent. When she hears Aunt Henrietta snoring, Caroline can turn on the tape."

"Then we'd have to tell Caroline," I said reluctantly. "What if she tattles?"

Tim thought about that. "She can't. If she lets us

44

do it, she'd be in trouble, too. And if she says no, we'll deny the whole thing."

We took the recorder and knocked on Caroline's door. She agreed immediately.

When I looked surprised at how easy it had been to convince her, she shrugged. "She's driving me crazy. This afternoon after school I was watching TV. Aunt Henrietta spent ten minutes telling me about all the chores she had to do when she was my age."

The sound of Aunt Henrietta's voice drifted up the stairs. "I think I'll go to bed," she was telling Mom.

"Here we go," Tim said. " 'Operation Get Rid of Aunt Henrietta' is about to begin."

"Be sure to wait until you hear her snoring," I said.

"Unlike you," Caroline said in a haughty voice, "I am not a dimwit."

Tim and I scurried back to our room just as Aunt Henrietta started up the stairs. We listened for a while, but Tim's room was too far down the hall for us to hear.

The next morning I was awake before the alarm even went off. I jumped in my clothes and hurried down for breakfast.

Aunt Henrietta was already at the table, calmly spreading jelly on her toast. "Good morning, Martin," she said brightly.

Tim staggered into the kitchen and plopped down in his chair.

"Did you sleep well?" I asked.

Tim gave me a look, but Aunt Henrietta smiled. "Like a baby," she answered.

I ran back upstairs and caught Caroline before she came down. "You didn't play the tape, did you?"

Caroline was holding her throat. "I did. We will have to do it more than once. What did you expect? That she'd be packing her bags, ready to go?" She brushed past me and continued downstairs.

"You look kind of pale this morning," Aunt Henrietta told Caroline. "Are you feeling well?"

"I'm all right," Caroline said.

"Your voice sounds scratchy," Dad said. "Does your throat hurt?"

"A little," she admitted.

Dad felt her head. "Better come in the office and let me take a look," he said.

Dad's office was at the back of our house. I followed them into his examining room, hoping I could help. Lately I've been thinking that I might like to be a doctor when I grow up. Dad switched on the lights and told Caroline to climb up on the examining table. He looked down her throat and took her temperature. "Hmmm," he said.

"What does that mean?" she asked nervously.

"I think we need to take out those tonsils," he said. "You had trouble all last winter, and they really look bad."

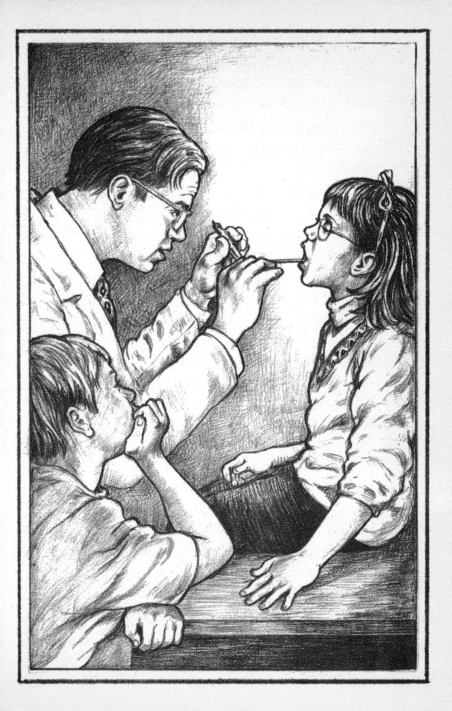

Caroline grabbed her throat with her hands. "You mean an operation?" she gasped. "It will hurt."

"Only a little," Dad said. He patted her back. "It's really not that bad. You won't even have to stay in the hospital overnight. It's certainly better than being sick all the time."

Then a worse thought struck me. "The first performance of the play is tonight," I said.

Dad shook his head. "Caroline's fever is a hundred and two. I'm sorry. The only place she is going is bed."

"I can't miss the play. Everyone is counting on me," Caroline wailed. "I've got one of the main parts."

"If we can get that fever down, you might be well enough to do the play tomorrow night and the Sunday matinee," Dad said as he gave Caroline some pills. I got her a drink of water and handed it to her. "But not tonight. Maybe someone else can do the part," Dad said.

"There isn't anyone," Caroline cried. "The whole play will be ruined. Everyone will hate me."

Dad hugged Caroline. "They won't hate you. You can't help being sick. Don't you have an understudy?"

Caroline blew her nose on the tissue Dad handed her. "I did. But she broke her leg in a bike accident!"

Dad made Caroline go to bed. When I passed her room a few minutes later, she was staring up at the ceiling, too unhappy to sleep. Dad told Mom the news, and a minute later she came into Caroline's room and felt her head. "How are you doing, honey?" she asked.

Caroline sat up. "Awful," she croaked. "It isn't fair. The whole play will be ruined—all because of my stupid tonsils. Nothing like this happens to other people."

"I missed the trip to the zoo last year when I had the chicken pox," I said.

"That's not the same," Caroline wailed. "Nobody hated you afterward."

"Marcia Stevens did," I said, grinning. "I gave them to her."

"It is a tough break," Mom agreed. "But no one is going to hate you for it. I'd better call someone at the Youth Theater."

"It's too late for anyone to learn my part," Caroline said.

"It's not that hard," I said without thinking. "I know it all from listening to you. I'll bet I know every word."

Caroline stared thoughtfully, making me realize what I had just said.

"Oh no," I said. "I'm not doing it. It's a girl's part."

"You and Caroline do look a little alike," Mom said. "You are almost the same size, so you could wear her costume."

"Absolutely not!" I shouted. "I'd have to kiss Willie Smith. I wouldn't care if you gave me a million dollars. I'm not doing it, and that's final."

7

To Kiss or Not to Kiss...

MOM HAD DECIDED to call Mrs. Stevens. She went downstairs to give her the bad news.

"You've got to do it," Caroline said. "Otherwise they'll have to cancel tonight's show."

I just shook my head.

Caroline changed her tune. "I wonder if Mom would like to hear about that tape and how kind you're being to Aunt Henrietta?"

"You wouldn't dare. You'd be in trouble, too."

"I don't think so," Caroline said. "I am awfully sick. And if I confess because I feel so bad for helping you..."

"I left a message," Mom announced as she came back into the room.

I glanced at Caroline. She smiled serenely and sank back on her pillow.

"I have to get ready for school," I said, backing out of the room. I brushed my teeth and scurried downstairs and out the front door.

Willie was nervous. I could tell because he just couldn't sit still. Miss Lawson scolded him several times. I decided it was best not to mention Caroline's problem. No need to get Willie upset. Maybe the grown-ups would have it solved by the time we got out of school.

During silent reading, Willie climbed up to the reading loft and sat beside me. He made jungle bird noises.

Miss Lawson peeked over the floor of the loft. "This is silent reading, Willie," she remarked. "You might find that a more interesting book if you read it right side up."

"Oops!" Willie said, turning the book. "I thought this was kind of a boring story."

"Perhaps we can forgive Willie for being so fidgety," Miss Lawson said to the rest of the class. "Tonight is the opening of the Youth Theater's production of *The Adventures of Tom Sawyer*, and Willie has the starring role. I dropped in at the dress rehearsal last night, and I can tell you it is a marvelous play. Several other students are in it, too. I hope you all are planning to see it."

At recess, Willie was still worried about kissing Caroline. I didn't tell him that he might be kissing someone else. "Just bend your head down and sort of kiss the air," I suggested. I puckered my lips and bent over to show him what I meant.

Two fifth-grade girls walked by. I turned the pucker into a whistle and bent over as if I were tying my shoe. "Fourth graders are soooo immature," one of them said.

"Good thinking," Willie said. "But next time you want to show me how to kiss, don't do it in school."

Caroline was bundled up on the couch watching television when I got home. "The surgeon can't do the operation for three more weeks," she said, sniffing. "That means it will be right before Valentine's Day."

I almost felt sorry for her. Then I remembered how she had threatened to tell about the tape. "Willie said when he had his tonsils out, the doctor just reached in and yanked them out," I teased.

"That's not true," Caroline gasped. "They put you to sleep. Willie doesn't even know what they did."

"Well, they did try to put him to sleep. But it didn't work. That happens sometimes, you know," I added wickedly. "Rrrip!"

"Mom!" Caroline screeched. "Martin's trying to scare me."

Mom came out of her study. She was frowning.

Just then I saw Mrs. Stevens's car pull up in our driveway.

"Why is she here?" I asked suspiciously.

"Well, she is the director of the play," Mom said. "We need to decide about what to do. We can't cancel the performance tonight. Every ticket has been sold. It's too late for anyone else to learn the part. But Mrs. Stevens thinks she's heard Caroline enough to do it. We've got the costume here."

"Oh no," Caroline groaned. "She'll ruin the whole play. She's too . . . old."

"There doesn't seem to be any other choice," Mom said. "Unless . . ." She looked at me hopefully.

"No!"

Aunt Henrietta had come into the living room. Even though I was saying no, I guess I already knew I was going to end up playing Becky Thatcher. I've only lived ten years, but there is one thing I've learned. A guy doesn't have a chance if a roomful of females want him to do something.

"I'm not kissing Willie Smith, no matter what," I said as Mrs. Stevens walked in the room. "And you have to promise that you won't tell anyone. And Caroline has to swear, too."

"Caroline has been so worried about the show that I'm sure she will promise," Mom said. "Tim will be out of town at his basketball game, so you don't have to worry about him teasing you."

Mrs. Stevens beamed at me. "I promise." She made a zipping motion with her lips. "Mum's the word," she said. She ran through the script with me to see if I really knew the part. "Oh, you are such a dear boy to do this," she said, practically gushing with relief. "Mayor Snodgrass, your children are just wonderful. You must be so proud of them."

Mom put her arm around my shoulder. "I am pretty proud of them. But we haven't got much time. We'd better try on the costume in case it needs to be altered."

I felt myself getting pale. I hadn't thought about that. Not only was I going to play a girl, I was going to have to dress like one. "Couldn't she be like a tomboy and wear jeans?" I pleaded.

"Girls didn't wear pants in those days," Mom answered.

"If you're going to do this thing, you might as well do it right," Aunt Henrietta put in. "Try to imagine yourself as a girl. Caroline's name is in the program. With a wig and some makeup, most people won't even know that it's not her."

"Do you think so?" I asked hopefully. "I wouldn't mind doing it so much if no one knew it was me."

"Let's see," Mom said. She pulled the dress over my head. Mrs. Stevens reached into a bag she had brought with her and produced a wig with long blond braids. Mom tugged it on and tucked in my own hair.

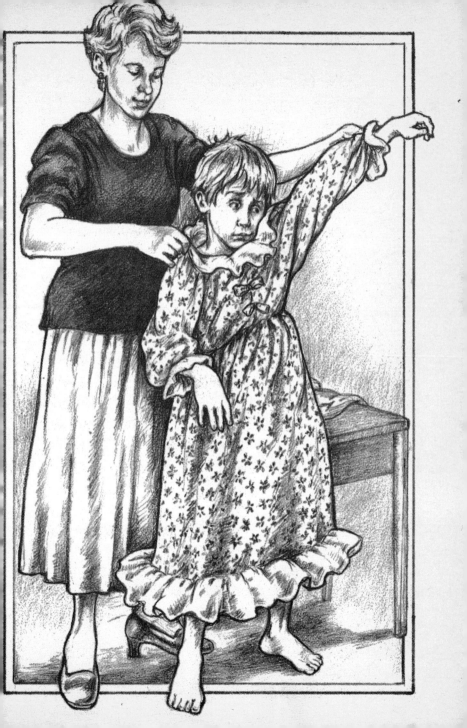

"It itches," I complained.

Mom looked thoughtful. "You don't really look like Caroline. But we might be able to convince them that you are somebody else. A cousin, perhaps. We could put makeup on to cover your freckles."

Mrs. Albright came into the living room to say good night. She was going out to dinner with Mr. DeWitt. She had agreed to stay with Caroline later while Mom and Dad went to the play.

"Could we borrow your name?" Mom asked.

"Agnes?" replied Mrs. Albright.

Mom nodded. "You could be Cousin Agnes from Columbus," she said to me.

Mrs. Stevens clapped her hands. "Oh, this is sooo much fun. I know just how we can do it, too. There is a small room next to the ticket window. Martin, you'll go to the green room with everyone else. They will all see you do your part. But instead of your going back to the green room, we'll say you are sick and had to go home. Then you go to the other room and change your clothes."

"Won't people wonder why Cousin Agnes is not in the green room?" I asked.

"Just say that she needs the time to look over her part, since she hasn't had a chance to practice," Aunt Henrietta suggested. "Actually, you probably could use the time to look over each scene."

For the next two hours everyone worked frantically

to turn me into Cousin Agnes. I had to practice walking and sitting like a girl. Robbie got up from his nap and watched. He liked my wig.

"Martin has new hair," he said, reaching up to pat it.

"It's pretend," I said. "I can take it off, see?"

Robbie tugged at his own hair. "Ow. Robbie's hair is stuck."

"That's real hair." I laughed.

Robbie stopped pulling his hair and patted the dress. "Martin has pretty dress. Like Mommy."

I groaned. "What if Robbie tells?"

"He'll forget all about it by tomorrow," Mom said. "If he says anything tonight, people will just think he's playing."

At last Mrs. Stevens looked at her watch. It was 5:30. "I'd better get home. Marcia will be worried."

I looked up in alarm. "Don't tell Marcia."

"I can't tell her that your cousin Agnes is filling in for Caroline?" she asked, giving me a big wink.

After she left, Mom helped me take off the dress. We ate a quick dinner. We had to be at the theater at 6:30, even though the play didn't start until 8:00 P.M. Caroline was huddled on the couch, feeling miserable, when I left. I felt sorry for her until she opened her mouth. "Don't mess up, dinosaur breath," she hissed.

When we arrived at the theater, Mom took the costume for "Cousin Agnes" into the small room Mrs. Stevens had mentioned. "Now remember, as soon as you are done with your part, say you are not feeling well and come here," she reminded me.

Willie already had his costume and makeup on when I walked into the yellow green room. "Hey, where's your sister?" he asked.

"She's sick," I explained. "Don't worry. Our cousin Agnes is coming from Columbus to take her part."

Willie looked as if he were about to explode. "Oh, man, everything will be ruined."

"Don't worry," I repeated soothingly. "Cousin Agnes knows the part. Really."

Willie still looked doubtful. "I never knew you had a cousin named Agnes," he said. "What is she like?"

"She, uh, is kind of a tomboy," I said.

"Is she cute?"

I gulped. "A little."

Willie sighed. "Good. Maybe it won't be so awful to kiss her." Then he gave me a suspicious look. "How come she knows the part?"

"Her school put on the same play and she was Becky Thatcher," I said, thinking quickly.

"I don't know," Willie said. "It's going to be pretty hard doing the play with someone new."

"Cousin Agnes is real easy to get to know," I said. "I'll bet after a few minutes you'll feel like she's an old friend."

8

Cousin Agnes

WILLIE WALKED ONTO the stage and poked his head through the stage curtains. "The theater is almost full. I don't see your family," he said.

"Dad and Aunt Henrietta are coming at the last minute," I said. "They didn't want Robbie to get restless waiting for the play to start. Mrs. Albright is staying home with Caroline. She and Mr. DeWitt will be here tomorrow night."

Willie tapped his foot anxiously. "Are you sure your cousin Agnes is coming? Columbus is pretty far."

"Don't worry," I said. "She'll be here."

"Why isn't she in the green room?" Willie asked.

I shrugged. "Maybe Mom is helping her with her costume."

Marcia Stevens came out on the stage with us. I could hardly recognize her with her wig and granny glasses. It made me feel better about being Cousin Agnes.

"Mom says it's almost time. I am sooo nervous," she confessed. "I heard about Caroline getting sick. I wish we could meet your cousin. Are you sure she'll know what to do? I hope I don't forget my lines."

"Marcia," I almost shouted when I could fit in a word, "you'll be great. Calm down. You're making me nervous listening to you."

I ran back to the green room. The prop lady handed me my fishing pole, the apple, and the straw hat. I took my shoes and socks off and rolled up my pants legs.

Mrs. Stevens scooted us all into position. The lights dimmed, and the orchestra played while the curtains slowly opened. The spotlight centered on a part of the stage made to look like a little house. Aunt Polly was scolding Tom. For the first few lines her voice sounded nervous. But then she seemed to forget about the audience, and her voice grew stronger as she told Tom he had to whitewash their picket fence. Marcia was great. She sounded just like a grouchy old lady. Willie was perfect, too. Tom picked up his brush, and the spotlight swung to the other side of the stage, where the fence and window box props were set up. He gave a loud unhappy sigh and started painting.

"You're on," said Mrs. Stevens, giving me a little push.

I did my part just right. The audience laughed when Tom finally gave in and allowed me to do his work for him. I picked up the brush and very carefully started painting the fence. Several other boys joined us, each one giving Tom a bribe.

The audience seemed to be enjoying the scene. Out of the corner of my eye I could see Dad, Robbie, and Aunt Henrietta in the very first row.

I only had a few minutes, while Aunt Polly admired the freshly painted fence and then the scenery was changed, to transform myself into Becky Thatcher. I raced past Carrie, one of the scenery changers. "I'm sick," I moaned. "I have to go home." I knew Carrie had a big mouth. In a few minutes everyone would think I had really left. I raced to the stage door. Then, at the last second, I swerved and slipped through the door next to the ticket window.

The room was somebody's office, with a desk and file cabinets along one wall. Mom jumped up from the only chair and threw the dress over my head. "We have to hurry," she said. She buttoned the dress in the back while I pulled on the wig and tucked my own hair underneath. Next Mom made me up.

"Hold still," she warned, "or these rosy cheeks will be on your forehead."

At last she slipped on my nose a pair of old-fashioned glasses without any glass in them and stood back, giving her creation a critical eye. "Hmm," she said. "Not bad."

I looked in the mirror. "Do I look like a girl?"

"I'd never guess it was you," Mom said.

"Really?" I asked.

Mrs. Stevens came to the door. "Hurry," she said. "You look wonderful," she added as we hurried back to the stage.

Finally we got to the scene where Tom and Becky Thatcher are in the schoolhouse, and Becky promises to marry Tom. I watched carefully to see if Willie recognized me, but I could see that he hadn't.

"Now that we're engaged," Tom finally said, "we have to seal it with a kiss."

I hid my face behind my apron and pretended to be bashful. "Please?" Tom said. "Just a little kiss?" Willie's face was blazing red, even through the makeup. This close, I was certain he would recognize me, but he was too embarrassed to look straight at me. Instead he stared at the bow in my hair.

I leaned forward to kiss the air, the way we'd practiced. I thought Willie was going to do the same. But at the last minute he must have decided to do it for real. He turned toward me just as I turned aside. Fortunately, our lips never met. Actually, it was our heads that met. We banged our heads together so hard that we both staggered back.

Willie recovered first. "Wow!" he said, thinking quickly. "That was a powerful kiss."

The audience roared with laughter. Willie leaned over and whispered, "Sorry, Agnes."

I couldn't believe it. Even this close, he didn't recognize me. This might be fun after all.

"That's quite all right, William," I said in a sugary voice.

The rest of the play went perfectly. At the end the whole cast came out to the front of the stage. Willie bowed first, and the audience clapped and cheered. Then it was my turn. "Hi, Martin," Robbie shouted as I walked to the edge of the stage in my dress and wig. I saw Dad trying to hush him, but luckily the clapping drowned out the sound of his voice before he said anything more.

I noticed Willie giving me a strange look as the rest of the cast took their bows, but I needn't have worried. After the show, he came running up to me. "You did a great job, Agnes."

"Thank you," I said, looking around for a way to make a quick escape.

"Do you think you will be here tomorrow?" he asked. He gave me a shy smile. Willie was flirting with me!

"Maybe Caroline will be better by tomorrow," I said quickly.

Mrs. Stevens came along and practically dragged us toward the theater lobby. "Everyone is waiting to congratulate the actors," she said.

Parents were crowding around the cast, telling

them what a good job they'd done. I squeezed my way to the small office, keeping my head down. Mom was waiting to help me change. "You did it," she said, hugging me. "You were terrific. Are you sure you don't want to just tell everyone it was you? You did such a good job."

I thought about it. "Willie was flirting with 'Agnes,'" I said. "I think that it's better for both of us if Agnes just goes home to Columbus and is never heard from again."

9

Girl Problems

ON SATURDAY AFTERNOON, Aunt Henrietta bundled up in a bright purple jogging suit and tied bows in her running shoes.

Caroline's fever was down. Dad had reluctantly agreed she could be in the play that evening, even though her voice still sounded scratchy. However, he insisted that she stay in bed until then. Tim was at another basketball game. His team had won five straight games. I figured he'd have another trophy pretty soon. At the rate he was piling up trophies, there wouldn't be space for me in his bedroom much longer. I was really tired of sleeping in there by now. Every time I passed my room and saw Aunt Henrietta's things in it, I felt unhappy. My desk was covered with papers because she was writing to all the relatives, asking them to attend the reunion. Her fuzzy pink bathrobe hung on my door, and my closet was full of her clothes.

"Coming with me?" she asked.

I hesitated. "I don't want to get tired out before the play."

"You youngsters today," Aunt Henrietta said with a shake of her head. "None of you has any pep. Why, when I was a girl, we had to run a mile just to get to the outhouse."

"Why don't you ride your bike," Mrs. Albright suggested. "You could put a leash on Sam and let him run with you."

"That sounds like a good idea," Aunt Henrietta said. "Sam won't bother me outside. It's only when I'm shut up in a room with a dog that I start sneezing."

I was trapped again. I went upstairs to get my coat. Robbie was in the bathroom. "Come see, Martin," he sang out proudly.

I checked to make certain no toys were in the toilet, then let him flush. Robbie watched as the water swirled down the drain. "All gone," he said proudly.

Robbie followed me downstairs. Aunt Henrietta was finishing her warm-up stretches. He and Aunt Henrietta barked at each other while I zipped up my coat and went next door to get Sam. Robbie was rolling on the floor giggling when I returned.

I rode my bike beside Aunt Henrietta as she jogged along, slowly at first, then faster and faster. Sam tugged at the leash, wanting to examine every bush. I had to pull the leash to keep up. Aunt Henrietta was tall and bony, but when she ran, she no longer looked awkward. She ran smoothly, her feet hardly seeming to touch the ground. She was smiling, and I could tell she really enjoyed running. Even riding a bike, I was already huffing by the time we started back, but Aunt Henrietta was hardly panting at all.

After a quick dinner, Mom drove Caroline and me to the theater. Mrs. Stevens made a big fuss about how nice it was to have Caroline back. The play was a big hit again, but on the ride home Caroline was fuming. "Everyone kept telling me how great 'Agnes' was in the play last night," she said.

"Martin did your part to help *you*," Mom reminded her.

"He didn't have to do it better than me," she stormed. "He's such a show-off."

There was one more performance Sunday afternoon, and luckily by that time no one was talking about "Cousin Agnes" anymore. The newspaper ran a story about the production. In addition to praising Willie's performance, the article said that Caroline was the perfect Becky Thatcher. Marcia was also singled out, and there was a lot of information about the Youth Theater.

Everyone was sad to see the curtain come down

on the last performance. We had a cast party, and the parent volunteers bought pizza for the cast, musicians, and crew. "I hope you will all try out next year," Mrs. Stevens said. There was a lot of talking and laughing, but no one wanted to leave. We had worked so hard, and now it was all over.

"Too bad Agnes had to miss this," Willie said.

"She said to tell you all good-bye," I lied smoothly.

"I liked her," Willie said. "She was real pretty."

"How could you tell with all that makeup she had on?"

"I could just tell," Willie said. He leaned close to me. "Did she say anything about me?"

"Er, no," I answered.

"Too bad," Willie said in his best Tom Sawyer voice. "I sure took a fancy to her."

Plays are sort of like Christmas, I found out. The best part is getting ready. For the next few days everyone talked about our play, but then it was forgotten until it seemed almost like a dream—although Willie kept asking when I was going to see Agnes. The weather had turned even colder and drearier. It snowed a few times, but not enough to be pretty or even to make a snowman. At school we divided up in groups to research different states. I was hoping to be in Brianne's California group. California seems to be a pretty interesting state. They were looking up things about the Gold Rush and pioneers and earthquakes. I was working with Steve and Lester, and our state was Iowa. I'll bet the people who live in Iowa like it fine, but it was not the most interesting state to have for a report.

Nothing had been said about Caroline's tonsils, and I think she was hoping Dad would just sort of forget about them. But then both of us got sick again and we missed almost a week of school. Dad scheduled her surgery for the Thursday before Valentine's Day.

When I got back to school, everyone was working on a relief map of the states. I found myself next to Willie. "Hasn't the tape worked yet?" he whispered.

I shook my head. "We've been playing it right along. This morning at breakfast, Aunt Henrietta was talking about how much she likes it here."

Marcia crumbled some brown paper to make the Rocky Mountains. She leaned close and gave me a smile as though we were sharing a big secret. "Are you talking about Valentine's Day? I am sooo excited. It's next week, you know."

Miss Lawson had already decorated the room with big paper hearts. Mrs. Headly, the art teacher, had promised to help us make boxes to hold the valentines. I thought that was a great idea. In third grade, valentines were just passed out. I had worried about Valentine's Day for weeks before the big day. I even had a nightmare about it. In my dream all the other kids had stacks of valentines on their desks. I didn't have a single one. Of course, it hadn't happened. But I was still glad that this year we all had our own boxes. That way no one would know who got the most valentines.

Now there were only a few days left. Valentine's Day was on a Sunday this year, but Miss Lawson had promised a party on Friday afternoon, and Marcia's mother was making cupcakes.

I had a feeling Marcia was expecting something special for Valentine's Day. The problem was that I wasn't sure I wanted to give something special to Marcia. Actually, I thought I might like to give something special to Brianne. On the other hand, I liked Marcia, and I didn't want to make her unhappy. Besides that, I wasn't even sure Brianne liked me. Or maybe she liked me the way I liked Marcia. It was confusing.

Finally I decided to ask Tim for advice. I figured he knew a lot about girls. Every night at least three girls called him. Tim acted as if that really bothered him. "Again?" he grumbled when the phone rang. Then he'd sigh and roll his eyes. But I noticed that he never refused to talk. As a matter of fact, he always took the phone and hid in the bathroom so no one could hear, and he was usually smiling when he came out.

"I'd just let them fight over me," Tim said. "May the best girl win."

"That's stupid. What if you don't like the winner?"

Tim shrugged. "Girls are all the same."

"They are not the same. Marcia likes everyone to follow the rules. She also likes dogs and sledding, and she can be lots of fun. Brianne is quiet and sweet, and she has a funny laugh."

Tim didn't seem to hear. He examined his lip in the mirror. "Does that look like hair to you?"

Caroline suddenly appeared at the door. I supposed she'd been listening all along. "Everyone has hair on their upper lip."

Tim looked again. "I think it looks thicker than usual."

Caroline peered closer. "Nope. Just baby fuzz," she said cheerfully.

Tim's face fell. "You can see it, can't you, Martin?"

I looked again. "Well, maybe a little."

Tim danced with glee. "I knew it. I'm probably going to have to shave pretty soon."

"Pretty soon, like in three years." Caroline snorted.

"Forget shaving," I said. "What about my problem?"

"At least you can tell the difference between girls," Caroline said, sounding almost friendly. "Tim here has been so busy playing sports the only thing he knows about girls is that they're not boys."

The next morning everyone brought a shoe box to art class and covered it with foil and red hearts. Then we cut a hole in the top of each.

"Now no one will know who gets the most valentines," Rochelle complained. Rochelle was the most popular girl in class, so she wanted everyone to see how many cards she got.

"I'm cutting the hole in my box extra big," Marcia said, "in case anyone gives me an extra-special valentine." She gave me a big smile.

Brianne was working at my table. She had made little lace hearts on the top of her box. "That looks nice," I said.

"Thank you," she said. "So does yours."

I looked at my box. All my hearts looked more like red lumps than hearts. "I'm not very good at making hearts," I said.

"I've got some left over." She handed me some perfectly shaped hearts.

She started to help me paste them on. Marcia gave me a lacy white heart. "Why don't you put this one on," she said, glaring at Brianne. "Then our boxes will match."

Art class ended while I was still deciding what to do. We went back to our room, and Mrs. Lawson gave us our spelling practice test. Next we had math. Every time I looked at Brianne, she was looking at me and smiling.

Miss Lawson wrote some problems on the board. I saw Jamie pass Charles a note, and Charles passed it to me.

Jessica told me that Brianne likes you.

Do you like her?
*Yes*_____ *No*_____

I checked the "Yes" and sent it back.

Willie was humming a beer commercial. Miss Lawson turned from the board, where she had been showing us how to subtract fractions. "Willie, are you paying attention?"

Willie nodded. "I can think better when I hear music."

"I don't believe that is true for everyone in the room," Miss Lawson said. "Although that might make an interesting experiment for science class."

I sighed with relief. She hadn't seen the note. Miss Lawson was pretty strict about notes. Any time she found one, she read it out loud.

Miss Lawson turned back to the board. Then she turned around suddenly. "By the way, Charles, you dropped the note you were passing," she said. She walked to his desk and held out her hand.

Charles reached under his desk and reluctantly handed her the note. Miss Lawson unfolded it.

"Unfortunately, the note isn't signed. But it seems to concern a rumor that Brianne likes someone. This certain someone returns your affection, Brianne."

Several of the boys whistled. Brianne slipped down in her seat and covered her face. I felt my face getting hot, but I stared at the ceiling and tried not to look guilty.

"Friday is our Valentine's party," Miss Lawson said. "Perhaps that would be a better time to express your feelings."

Marcia twisted around in her seat and stared at me. I pretended to concentrate on fractions.

After lunch, Marcia was waiting for me on the playground. "Brianne was really embarrassed about that note," she said.

I nodded, dreading the next question.

"Who wrote it?"

"I'm not sure," I said truthfully.

"It must have been Charles," Marcia said. "The note was under his desk."

Luckily for me, Willie ran over to us at that very minute. "Hey, Snodgrass. Do you think your cousin Agnes will be here on Valentine's Day?"

"I-I don't think so," I stammered. "She doesn't come very often."

"Well then, could you give me her address? I want to send her a valentine," Willie said.

"I think it's unlisted," I said.

Willie stared at me. "Your cousin has an unlisted address?"

I thought frantically. "Her father is like an undercover investigator. He's probably put a lot of people in jail. So they have to be careful. No one is allowed to know their address."

Willie whistled. "Wow! You sure have a lot of interesting people in your family."

Willie was so impressed with my story that it made me feel guilty. But it was better than telling him he had almost kissed me.

Willie leaned close and whispered, as though telling a secret, "Are you sure you couldn't give it to her? It's really pretty. Lots of mushy lace and stuff."

I felt my face growing red. "Did you really like her that much? You only saw her for one play."

Willie held his hand over his heart. "That was enough. From the first moment I was in love. And when we kissed . . ."

My face was blazing. "Wait a minute. You didn't kiss. You bumped heads, remember?"

"How did you know that?" Willie asked. He was smiling broadly.

"Er, my cousin told me," I said.

Willie suddenly burst out laughing. "Was that before or after you put on the dress?"

"You knew all this time?"

"You should see how red your face is." Willie started laughing so hard he could only nod. Finally he stopped laughing long enough to say, "You fooled me for a few minutes. I was pretty suspicious, though. Then when Robbie yelled your name, I knew for sure. Actually, I had a little talk with Robbie one day when I was at your house. He told me all about your 'pretend' hair."

By the end of the day everyone knew that I had been Agnes. Surprisingly enough, although everyone teased me about believing Willie was in love with Agnes, no one said anything awful about my acting the part of a girl. I had done all that worrying about getting caught for nothing.

Mr. DeWitt was sitting on his porch petting his cat, Daffy, when I got off the school bus. "Did you come to see Sam?" he asked.

"Actually, I wanted to talk to you," I said. I let Sam out of the house for a romp and sat down next to Mr. DeWitt.

Mr. DeWitt picked up a seed catalog from the table beside his chair. "Are we going to plant a garden this year?" Mr. DeWitt asked. Last summer he had helped me grow a prize-winning pumpkin for the fair.

"Sure," I said. Then I sighed.

"You are looking pretty glum," Mr. DeWitt remarked.

"I have girl trouble," I admitted. "Marcia Stevens thinks I'm her boyfriend. She's expecting a really fancy valentine. But I sort of like a girl named Brianne."

"And you want to give her a fancy valentine," Mr. DeWitt finished for me. "Why don't you give them both one?"

"Then Marcia will be mad," I said glumly. "This boyfriend stuff is hard. I like Marcia. She's the one who gave me Sam. I just wish I didn't have to be her boyfriend."

Mr. DeWitt shook his head. "Hmm. You do have a problem. Have you tried explaining this to Marcia?"

I shook my head. "She'd be mad."

"Well, I have generally found it's best to be truthful with people."

"Maybe I should give them both a nice card, but not sign my name on Brianne's," I said thoughtfully.

"You mean like signing it from 'your secret admirer'?"

"That's a great idea," I said.

Mr. DeWitt stroked Daffy's soft fur.

"I wish I could figure out some way to make Marcia not want to be my girlfriend," I said.

"You'll have to figure that one out yourself," Mr. DeWitt answered.

"Did you get Mrs. Albright a valentine?" I asked.

Mr. DeWitt nodded. "I got her a big mushy one. And a box of chocolates."

"I'll bet she'll like that," I said.

"I hope so," he said.

Sam bounded across the yard and up on Mr. DeWitt's porch. He sniffed Daffy, wanting to play. Daffy hunched up her back and hissed. She growled low in her throat. Sam just wagged his tail.

"I don't think Daffy likes Sam." I laughed. I took Sam inside Mr. DeWitt's house and gave him his supper.

"Good luck with your problem," Mr. DeWitt called after me as I walked back to my own house.

I sighed. I had a feeling I needed more than good luck to solve this problem.

10

Tonsils and Toy Soldiers

MOM AND DAD took Caroline to the hospital very early Thursday morning.

"It's not that bad," I said when I saw her scared look. "Willie told me that when he had his tonsils out he got to eat all the ice cream he wanted."

Caroline made a face. "I don't even like ice cream," she said.

"You ought to tell the doctor to put your tonsils in a jar," Tim joked. "Then you could take them to school for show-and-tell."

Caroline rolled her eyes. "Oh, and wouldn't that make me the most popular girl in school." She pretended to be flirting. "Come on over here, handsome, and I'll show you some pickled tonsils."

"I'd think it was interesting," I said.

"Me too," Tim said.

Caroline looked back with a withering glance as she walked out the door. "Of course *you* two would."

"Poor Caroline," I said after she left. "She's going to miss Valentine's Day."

I followed Tim to the kitchen. "That's baby stuff," he said. "We don't do that in seventh grade." He rummaged though the cupboards looking for something to eat. "I wish Mrs. Albright hadn't taken the day off."

"She's going to Columbus with Mr. DeWitt," I said. "He's going to take her to the art museum and then to a show."

I took two bowls out of the cupboard and put them on the table. "You're lucky you don't have to worry about valentines," I said. "I have to buy two fancy ones."

Aunt Henrietta bustled into the kitchen just as Tim started to pour cereal into a bowl. She was wearing the fuzzy pink robe and slippers. She looked sleepy. "Wait," she said. "I promised your mother I'd fix breakfast."

"We like cereal," Tim said.

"No, no," she fussed. "Breakfast is the most important meal of the day. Now, you two go get ready for school. By the time you are done, I'll have something ready."

"If Mrs. Albright marries Mr. DeWitt, I'll bet Aunt Henrietta will stay forever," Tim whispered glumly as we climbed the stairs.

Robbie jumped off the toilet as we walked in the bathroom.

"I went," he said proudly. He suddenly looked guilty. "I flush now."

"Wait," I yelled. I checked to make sure there was nothing that shouldn't be flushed. Sure enough, a little toy soldier settled slowly to the bottom.

"He wants to go round and round," Robbie said, reaching for the handle.

I grabbed his hand away. "It will plug up the toilet," I scolded. "What are we going to do?" I asked Tim.

"I'm not reaching in there," Tim said, wrinkling his nose.

"Well, I'm not either." I sighed and said, "I'll go tell Aunt Henrietta."

I carried Robbie downstairs and explained the problem to Aunt Henrietta. I expected her to yell, or at least act upset. Instead, she chuckled and said, "That little rascal is sure stubborn." Then she calmly put on a disposable plastic glove and bounded upstairs.

Now that the crisis was over, I went back upstairs and got ready for school. By the time I helped Robbie get dressed and was back in the kitchen, Tim was already sitting at the table.

"I decided cereal would be all right," Aunt Henrietta said, "if we dressed it up a little." She had sliced bananas on the cereal, and there was a plate of bacon and another with warm blueberry muffins.

She poured us some orange juice, fixed Robbie's breakfast, and sat down.

"This looks good," Tim said. He wolfed down two blueberry muffins before I'd even poured milk on my cereal.

Aunt Henrietta smiled. "We are starting to get answers back from relatives who are coming to the reunion," she remarked. "Your cousins John and Vickie are coming all the way from Seattle."

"Do they have any kids?" I asked.

"I remember them," Tim said. "They stayed overnight one time. You were too little to remember. Cousin John snored so loud the house shook. They had a boy named Jason. He broke all my crayons."

"I don't think I have them on the family tree," I said. I'd hung the paper on the refrigerator, the way Marcia had hers, and I'd been filling in all the names I'd heard.

Aunt Henrietta peered at the tree. "I'm not sure they would even fit. John's father was the son of your grandfather's brother. So John is your father's first cousin, once removed, and your second cousin."

I shook my head. "It's hard to keep track of everyone. I never knew I was related to so many people."

"There are a lot of us," Aunt Henrietta agreed.

"Are Matt, Corey, and Tabitha coming?" I asked, naming our cousins from a nearby town.

Aunt Henrietta consulted her list. "Their parents

were some of the first to accept," she said.

Tim stuffed a last bit of bacon in his mouth. "Matt is pretty good at sports, too. Maybe we can organize some contests."

I looked at the long list of names that had accepted the invitation and sighed. I could picture it all now. It wasn't bad enough to live in a family of fabulous people. Now I was going to spend a whole weekend with fifty more of them.

"I didn't know it was so late," said Tim as he slid back his chair and grabbed his book bag. "I'm going to miss my bus." He dashed out the door. Through the window I saw the bus come to a stop just as he made it to the end of the drive.

I picked up another blueberry muffin. "Is there anyone in our family who is just ordinary?" I asked.

"I am," Aunt Henrietta answered cheerfully.

"You're not ordinary. You've lived all over the world."

"I have lived in some pretty interesting places," Aunt Henrietta said. "But I was just a schoolteacher. That is not *extra*ordinary." She smiled. "And I always wanted to do something extraordinary. I guess that's why I want to be in the Boston Marathon."

I gulped down my milk. It was almost time for my bus. "Do you think you will win?" I asked.

Aunt Henrietta chuckled. "I'm about forty years too late for that. I'll be happy if I just finish."

11

Be My Valentine

CAROLINE WAS JUST getting home when I arrived after school. She looked tired and pale and didn't answer when I asked how she felt. Mom helped her upstairs to bed.

"She doesn't feel much like talking," Dad said. "Her throat will be pretty sore for the next couple of days."

Tim walked in and overheard what Dad said. "Hooray," he exclaimed. "Two days without listening to Caroline."

I felt like cheering, too, but the stern look Dad gave Tim made me change my mind.

"Dad, can you drive me to the drugstore to get some valentines? The party is tomorrow," I reminded him.

"Why did you wait until now to ask?" Dad asked, throwing his arms up in the air.

"It's my fault," Mom said as she came downstairs. "He asked me two weeks ago. Dad needs to get back to his office, Martin, but we can go while Caroline is asleep."

Mom took me to the drugstore and I looked through the boxes on display. There wasn't much of a choice. I sighed, thinking about how easy it had been to choose when I was younger. But now I discarded box after box.

"These are nice," Mom said. She held up a box of superhero ones.

"Too babyish," I grumbled.

"Well, how about these?" Mom suggested.

I looked at them. "Too mushy."

I finally found an assortment of funny ones that seemed all right. "I have to buy a fancy card, too," I said as I started hunting through the rack.

Mom held up a pretty card. "Marcia would like this one," she said.

"It's not for Marcia," I mumbled. I had decided that if I didn't give Marcia a special valentine, she'd get the message.

"Oh." Mom looked surprised.

Just then I saw the perfect card. It had a glittering red heart. *From your secret admirer,* read the words on the front, just as Mr. DeWitt had said. I grabbed it before Mom could ask any more questions.

We bought some candy hearts to slip a treat into everyone's envelopes, then headed home.

Usually Mom helped me with my valentine cards. She would write each name on the envelope while I wrote *From Martin* on the card. But this year she was too busy running upstairs tending to Caroline. Now I had all these cards to finish in one night, plus a science test to study for. I also had a book report due in two days, and I hadn't even finished half the book. With a sigh I sat down with the list of names Miss Lawson had sent home.

"Would you like some help?" Aunt Henrietta asked. When I nodded gratefully, she picked up the list and started writing the names on the envelopes in her thin and spidery handwriting.

"Did you have valentines when you were in school?" I asked as we worked.

Aunt Henrietta read one of them and chuckled. "Not like these." She pointed to the card I'd picked out for Brianne. "What name do you want on this card?"

I grabbed the envelope. "I'll do that one," I said.

I looked through the pile of valentines for one to give Marcia. None of them seemed quite right.

"You haven't picked a card for Marcia," Aunt Henrietta said, checking the list.

"I think I will make her one," I said.

Aunt Henrietta's eyebrow went up a notch, but she

didn't say anything. She went upstairs and came back with a large white envelope. "You won't be able to fit a homemade card in those dinky envelopes," she said, pointing to the remaining boxed cards.

I stuffed the other envelopes in a paper bag and took a piece of colored paper to my room. First I drew a large heart. It turned out crooked, as mine usually did, but I guessed it didn't matter. I tapped my pencil against my teeth while I thought. Finally I wrote:

> *Violets are blue,*
> *Roses are pink,*
> *I'd be your valentine*
> *If your feet didn't stink.*

Perfect. Marcia would probably never speak to me again. I tried not to think about the day Marcia had let me pick out Sam, and the fun we'd had sledding. I slipped the card into Aunt Henrietta's envelope and stuffed it into my sack.

The next morning I rode my bike to school so I could be there early. I did a quick check around the playground as I parked my bike in the rack. I was in luck. There was no sign of Brianne or Marcia. But I had to hurry. Already the playground was starting to fill up.

"You are very early this morning," Mr. Higgenbottom, the principal, said as I walked through the door.

"I, er, wanted to pass out these valentines," I said.

"Hey, Snodgrass," a voice said behind me. Mr. Higgenbottom frowned. Willie Smith was not his favorite person.

Willie held up an old beat-up sack and brushed off some streaks of dried mud. "Almost lost my valentines," he said cheerfully. "I dropped them while I was riding my bike."

Mr. Higgenbottom stared suspiciously after us as we walked down the hall. Miss Lawson was already in the room. "Good morning, boys. I was just going to the storage room to get the video player. I have a movie for the party this afternoon. Martin, do you suppose you could help me?"

I hesitated. "It will only take a few minutes," Miss Lawson said.

Willie was passing out his cards. I handed him my cards. "Will you pass these out for me? The big white envelope is for Marcia."

"Sure," Willie said, grabbing the sack.

I followed Miss Lawson to the storage room. It was locked, and we had to find the custodian to get the key. By the time we got back to our room, all the other kids were there, and it was almost time for the bell.

"Don't worry," Willie said. "I passed yours out. I figured the other big envelope was for Brianne, right?"

I nodded gratefully. "Thanks," I said.

Willie pulled a slightly grimy card out of his back pocket. "I bought this fancy card to tease you about 'Agnes.' But now I'll just throw the envelope away and give the card to somebody else."

"Martin, could you go back and ask the custodian for an extension cord?" Miss Lawson asked.

"Sure," I said. I ran down and got the cord. By the time I returned, the bell had already rung. Willie was in his seat making a paper airplane out of the old envelope. I wondered who had gotten "Agnes's" card.

"This afternoon we'll have our party and you can open your cards," Miss Lawson said. "But this morning we are going to review for our social studies quiz."

Willie let out a loud war cry: "Ahh, ahh, ahh!"

Mrs. Lawson frowned. "I don't think that will be on the test, Willie. But perhaps you could tell us what kind of houses the Iroquois people built."

Willie grinned. "Longhouses. They were made out of logs, and more than one family lived inside."

"Very good," Mrs. Lawson said.

Finally it was time for the party. Mrs. Stevens delivered the cupcakes, and another mother brought some punch. Everyone opened their boxes and looked through their valentines. I had just taken a big bite of my cupcake when Marcia came over to my desk. I gasped. She was smiling. And she was holding the fancy card. "Oh, Martin," she said. "You are so romantic. Every time I start thinking you don't like me anymore, you do something nice like this."

My stomach did a weird flip-flop. Willie had put the fancy card in Marcia's box. That meant that Brianne must have the other one. I realized I hadn't written a name on either envelope, and that both cards had big white envelopes. I groaned and put my head on my desk.

"Are you sick?" Marcia asked. "Do you want me to tell Miss Lawson?" She sounded worried.

I sat up. "I just have a little headache," I said. "I'm glad you liked it," I managed to choke out. Out of the corner of my eye I could see Brianne glaring at me.

Marcia hung around almost the whole party. She even sat next to me during the movie. Miss Lawson had gotten *The NeverEnding Story*. It was one of my favorites, but I couldn't concentrate. I looked over at Brianne. She was sitting very close to Willie, and they were laughing.

"Did you see the pretty card Willie gave Brianne?" Marcia whispered. "It was almost as nice as the one you gave me. He must really like her."

We took a break in the middle of the movie. Willie sauntered over. "Marcia must have really liked her card," he remarked.

"Why did you give it to *her*?" I said.

Willie looked surprised. "Wasn't that who it was

for? You were worried about getting her something special."

I nodded glumly. Willie didn't seem to notice how miserable I was.

"Brianne liked 'Agnes's' card, too," he went on happily. He pulled his too-short shirtsleeves down to cover his knobby wrist bones. "Brianne smells like vanilla. Did you ever notice?"

12

More Tonsils

ALL WEEKEND, CAROLINE kept everyone in the house running to wait on her. Mom coaxed her to eat with ice cream, Jell-O, and other goodies. Caroline talked only in whispers and tried to convince everyone she was practically at death's door.

Monday was a rainy day. It was a cold dreary rain. A layer of fog drifted a few feet off the ground, and the sky was dark and gloomy. All day I felt miserable and cranky. Usually the first thing I did when I got home after school was to play with Sam. But today all I could think of was how nice it would be to curl up on the couch with a cup of cocoa and watch TV.

When I walked in the door, I saw that Caroline had beaten me to it. She was tucked up on the couch sipping cocoa and watching some dumb soap opera.

"Could I have some cocoa, too?" I asked Mrs. Albright.

"I'm sorry, dear. I just made the last of it for Caroline. How about a glass of orange juice?"

It didn't sound as good as cocoa, but I accepted a glass and took a sip. It tasted good, but my throat burned when I swallowed.

"Where is Mom?" I asked.

Mrs. Albright put the juice container back in the refrigerator. "She couldn't stay away from the office any longer. She went to pick up some papers. Your aunt went with her."

From upstairs we could hear the sound of Robbie jumping in his crib. That was his way of letting us know he was awake from his nap. Mrs. Albright went upstairs to get him, and I wandered back into the living room.

"Let's watch something else on TV," I suggested.

"I suppose you'd rather watch cartoons," Caroline sneered. "That's about right for your brain."

On the screen two people were kissing. "I suppose you have to be pretty smart to watch that," I said.

"Look, dog breath," Caroline croaked, "I'm sick, so I get first choice."

"I heard your tonsils were so big and ugly they are going to put them in a museum so everyone can come and look at them," I said.

"I'm going to tell Mom and Dad you were mean to me when I was sick," she yelled, her voice suddenly stronger.

"So you *can* talk. Maybe I'll tell Mom and Dad you've been faking," I said.

"I haven't been faking," she said. There were tears in her eyes. "I've been sick, and you've been having all the fun."

"What fun?" I sputtered.

"I didn't even get to go to my class's Valentine's party."

"Believe me, you didn't miss that much," I said. My head hurt when I moved it.

Dad poked his head around the corner. I was surprised to see him. Usually he was in his office this time of day, seeing patients.

"It's a little slow this afternoon," Dad said. "I thought I'd slip over and check on Caroline."

Robbie toddled in. He was holding his throat. Ever since Caroline had come home, Robbie had been worried about her. "Caroline hurt," he announced gravely.

Dad pulled Robbie up on his lap. "Caroline's all right," he explained for about the tenth time. "She just had her tonsils out."

Robbie kept holding his throat. He gave Dad a suspicious look. "No hurt Robbie," he warned.

"No, no," Dad said. "You have good tonsils."

"Tonsils?" Robbie asked.

"Come over here, Martin," Dad said. "Maybe if Robbie can see your tonsils, he'll understand."

Obligingly I opened my mouth.

"Hmm," Dad said. "Hmm."

I didn't like the sound of Dad's "hmm." "What's wrong?" I asked.

"Is your throat sore?"

"A little," I admitted.

"Your tonsils look worse than Caroline's did. I think we need to take yours out, too."

A smile spread slowly across Caroline's face. "Now you'll see I wasn't faking."

Tim walked in just in time to hear Caroline's last remark. "Who's faking?" he asked.

"No one. Martin has to have his tonsils out, too," Caroline crowed.

"Tough luck," Tim said, giving me a friendly jab on the arm. "I'm glad I had mine out when I was little."

"What's the point of having tonsils if they just have to come out," I grumbled.

"Tonsils filter out germs," Dad explained. "We really don't like to take them out. But when they get infected and make you sick all the time, then it's best."

"Does it really hurt that bad?" I asked Caroline.

She smiled sweetly. "It's awful."

"It's not much worse than a sore throat," Dad said.

That was pretty easy for him to say. He wasn't the one that was going to feel it. Caroline grabbed her throat and made a terrible face when he wasn't looking. "It really hurts," she mouthed.

Tim looked around. "Where's Aunt Henrietta?"

"She went to town with Mom," Caroline said.

"Whew," Tim said. "I was afraid I would have to go running."

Dad glanced through the mail Mrs. Albright had stacked on the hall table. "Looks as if several more relatives have accepted our invitation. Here's one from Aunt Judith."

"Why do we have to have this stupid reunion anyway," I grumbled.

"In the past, people often stayed close to the places where they grew up. I think it gave them a sense of belonging. You understood your roots," Dad said seriously. "But today most families are so spread out that sometimes even close relations don't know one another. Look at our family, scattered all over the country."

I thought about the family tree Miss Lawson had given us. With Aunt Henrietta's help, most of the names were filled in. There were a few relatives I had never even met. Maybe it would be interesting to see some of those people. It was kind of nice to think about a family being a giant tree with branches growing clear across the country.

"Where are all these people going to stay?" I asked.

"We are reserving rooms at several motels," Dad said. "And a couple of people said they would bring camping trailers. Aunt Jane and Uncle Dave said they would pitch a tent in the yard. Thank heavens we have such a big yard."

Our house had a huge yard in front with lots of shady trees. The back was big, too, and it was surrounded on two sides by a cornfield.

"We could set up our tent," I suggested.

"That's a great idea. If you kids slept in the tent, we could put up a few more people in the house," Dad said. "We'll put the tents in the front yard, kind of off to the side. That way we can have the tables and chairs in the front yard and you kids can have the backyard for games."

Caroline looked out the window. "I hope it's warmer than this," she said just as Mom and Aunt Henrietta came in the door.

Aunt Henrietta folded her umbrella. "It *is* awful outside. I guess I won't be running today."

"I'll bet weather like this makes you wish you didn't live here," Caroline said.

Aunt Henrietta shook her head. "Oh no," she said. "I love it here. It's the strangest thing. A week or two ago I was getting homesick. But now I think I'd like to stay." She looked straight at me. "Sometimes I hear this little voice in my head."

"L-little voice?" I stammered.

98

"It keeps saying, 'Stay, stay. Make this your home forever.'" She smiled innocently. "Isn't that peculiar?"

I gulped. "That is strange," I agreed.

13

Capitals and Sympathy

CAROLINE GAVE ME the tape back the next morning. "She knows," she hissed. "You'd better get rid of this before Mom and Dad find out."

"I think Caroline is right," Tim said. "It was nice of her not to tell."

"I wonder why it didn't work," I said.

"Because you thought of it, dimwit," Caroline said with a sneer.

Tim looked at me and winked. "I see having tonsils out doesn't improve your personality."

Caroline sniffed. "Neither does living with bird-brains," she said as she flounced off to get ready for school.

I had to get ready for school, too. Dad had given

me some medicine. He said I wouldn't need to miss school, since I didn't have a fever. "Good news," he had announced that very morning at breakfast. "The surgeon can fit you in this Friday."

"Caroline got to wait three weeks," I whined.

"She had all that time to think about it," Dad said. "You'll just have it done quickly and it will be over. Since we are doing it on Friday, you won't even have to miss that much school."

I was feeling pretty glum when I went to school. It was hard to concentrate. Miss Lawson gave us a map and we had to fill in the names of the states. We had to memorize all the capitals. Then she let us divide into groups to quiz each other.

I was in a group with Brianne, Willie, Jason, and Marcia. Brianne sat close to Willie and didn't even look at me. They were holding hands under the table so Miss Lawson couldn't see them.

"What's the capital of New York?" Jason asked.

"Albino," Willie shouted.

Everyone laughed. "Albany," Marcia corrected. "That's so easy, since our town is New Albany."

"Oh," Willie said with a shrug. "I knew it was something that started with an *A*."

"I have to have my tonsils out," I announced.

Willie grabbed his throat, clowning around. "Arrgg," he gasped. He forgot he was holding Brianne's hand. He jerked his hand so fast that she was pulled off her seat. She teetered against him for a second. Then her chair fell over and both of them landed on the floor.

Miss Lawson was there in an instant. She did not look happy. "Willie and Brianne, would you please explain to me how two people can fall on the floor quizzing each other on state capitals?"

"It was all my fault," Willie said gallantly. "I got dizzy."

Miss Lawson looked tired. "Dizzy," she repeated.

Willie nodded. "I was so dizzy I fell into Brianne's chair and knocked her over."

"Perhaps you need to explain your dizzy spells to Mr. Higgenbottom," Miss Lawson said.

"It was my fault," I said. "I told him that I was going to have my tonsils out. Willie always gets dizzy when he hears about blood."

A smile twitched the corners of Miss Lawson's mouth. "Let's keep the conversation to state capitals. Maybe we can discuss tonsils in science class."

"Thanks," Willie whispered when Miss Lawson went back to her desk. "Mr. Higgenbottom said if he saw me one more time this year, I was in big trouble."

"Are you scared about having your tonsils out?" Marcia asked at recess.

"No," I said. "Well, maybe a little bit. My sister said it was awful."

"I had mine out last year," she said. "It wasn't really that bad. You just feel like you have a sore throat afterward. I could come over and make you some Jell-O."

"Mrs. Albright will make me some," I said. Then, seeing her disappointed look, I added, "That was nice of you to offer."

"How is Sam?" she asked.

I shrugged. "He's getting used to staying at Mr. DeWitt's house. I take him out a lot."

"You could bring him over sometime to visit his mother, Mitzi," Marcia said.

"Maybe," I said.

Marcia was the only one who was worried about me. You would think that someone facing surgery on Friday would get a little attention. But no. Mom was all upset over the meetings about the new highway. "I just don't know which side to take," she said at dinner. "One group would like the highway built because it would cut down on all the big trucks going through town. And they are right. The traffic is getting horrible and some streets are just too narrow for big trucks. But the other group says that all the shopkeepers in town would lose business because everyone would just pass by. And they are right, too. It doesn't matter which side I take, I'm going to make people unhappy."

In addition, there was the family reunion, which

was being held on Easter weekend. So far fifteen families had accepted. "Most people are off work, and the weather is usually pretty good," Mom had explained. "So the out-of-town people will be able to stay longer." She and Aunt Henrietta were busy making arrangements at motels and ordering food.

"We will have to figure out bathroom schedules, and we need lots of activities for the children," Mom said at dinner.

"Dad said I could organize some baseball games," Tim said. He rolled his eyes at me. "Most kids like to play baseball."

"Scavenger hunts!" Caroline suggested. "I could write some clues."

"Doesn't anyone care about me?" I exploded. "I have to have my tonsils out, and all anyone talks about is highways and baseball games."

There was a moment of shocked silence. "Oh, honey, we didn't know you were that upset about it," Mom said.

"It's no big deal," Caroline said breezily.

"Oh yeah," I retorted. "Then why did you make such a big fuss?"

"Dr. Michael will do the surgery," Dad said. "But I'll be right there watching."

"I'll bring you some ice cream afterward," Tim promised.

"I have an idea," Caroline said. "After dinner, let's

play Monopoly. You always win that. It will keep your mind off it."

Even Aunt Henrietta started telling me a funny family story, trying to cheer me up. It was almost embarrassing. A minute earlier I was unhappy because I wasn't getting any attention. Now I was getting too much. But that's the way it is with families, I guess. Sometimes they are a pain, but they are great when you need them.

14

Tonsils Again

FRIDAY MORNING CAME all too soon. "You are lucky," Willie had said on Thursday.

"Lucky?" I hadn't been able to believe my ears.

"You don't have to take the test on state capitals," Willie said.

"Ha," I said. "Miss Lawson will just make me take it when I get back."

"Well, at least you get a few days off school," Willie said.

"I'll tell you what," I said. "I'll go to school and you go get your tonsils out."

It was hard to feel lucky as I got ready to leave for the hospital. We were supposed to be there at seven in the morning, and I wasn't allowed to have breakfast. Dad explained that food might make me sick when they put me to sleep.

"But I'm starving," I complained. As if to prove it, my stomach made a funny little growl.

As soon as we arrived at the hospital, a lady at the desk put a plastic bracelet on me. Then we were taken upstairs to a room with a bed. A nurse handed me a white gown. It had babyish little teddy bears on it. "That's our most fashionable outfit," she said when I frowned.

I didn't have time to think about it because as soon as I had changed, another nurse came in and gave me a shot. "Is that going to put me to sleep?" I asked nervously.

The nurse smiled. "It might make you a little sleepy. Mostly it will just help you relax."

Dad patted my head. "I'm going to go change and get ready to help Dr. Michael," he said. "I'll see you in a few minutes."

There was a television in my room. Mom and I watched while we waited, but that early in the morning there wasn't anything interesting on. "There is one good thing," I said. "I always wanted to see the inside of the operating room. I want to see if it's like the ones they show on TV."

At last I was wheeled into the operating room. I saw Dad with a mask on his face. Dr. Michael was there, and so was another doctor. "This is Dr. Abrams," Dad said.

Dr. Abrams explained that he was the one who would put me to sleep.

I tried to sit up, but he gently pushed me back down. "You won't let them do anything until you're sure I'm asleep, will you?" I asked.

"I promise," he said. "I'm going to give you a little shot. You just relax."

"All right," I said. "But remember. Pinch me or something. Make sure I'm really, really asleep." I took two quick breaths.

"I'm not asleep yet," I mumbled. My mouth tasted awful, and my throat hurt.

"Oh, you're awake," said a nurse, peering down at me. "Good."

"I haven't gone to sleep yet," I croaked. "Don't let them do it."

The nurse chuckled. "It's already done. It's all over."

I tried to focus my eyes, but I was too sleepy. "I forgot to look at the operating room," I muttered as I fell back to sleep.

The next time I woke up, I was back in the first room and Mom was sitting in a chair beside me. "Thirsty," I whispered.

Mom gave me some little pieces of ice to suck on. My throat felt terrible.

"When you're more awake, we can go home," she said. Her hand felt cool on my head. I nodded. As long as I didn't talk, my throat didn't hurt too bad.

After a couple of hours the doctor checked me and said I could go home.

I was surprised that it was so late. Tim and Caroline were already home from school and waiting for me. "How was it?" Tim asked.

I shook my head and pointed to my throat.

"He doesn't want to talk now," Caroline told Tim in her bossy voice.

For once she was right. All I wanted to do was sleep. Mom helped me to bed, and the next thing I knew, it was Saturday morning.

All day I sat bundled up on the couch and read or watched TV. Mrs. Albright brought me some ice cream. I was really getting hungry, but I only managed to swallow two tiny bites.

At three o'clock the doorbell rang. "There's someone to see you," Mom said.

"Is it Willie?" I whispered.

"No. It's Marcia," Mom said. "She says she has something for you."

I groaned. What could she want? Then I realized I was still wearing my pajamas. I pulled the covers up under my chin so she couldn't see.

Marcia came in the room carrying a small bowl with a lid. "I know you don't feel like talking," she said. "But I brought you something." She took off the lid. "It's vanilla pudding. I made it myself."

I looked in the bowl. It looked kind of watery.

Marcia made a face. "It's the cooked kind. It didn't get quite hard enough. But I thought it might feel good on your throat."

"Thank you," I croaked. "It looks really good."

We sat there a minute in silence. "Are you cold?" Marcia asked, pointing to my blanket.

I gave a weak nod.

"I could take Sam for a walk before I go home," she offered.

"He would like that." I looked at the pudding. "Could you ask Mrs. Albright for a spoon?"

Marcia went to the kitchen and came back with a spoon. "You don't have to eat it if you don't want it," she said.

"No, I want to," I said. I didn't really, but I knew her feelings would be hurt if I didn't. To my surprise, the pudding slid down smooth and cool on my throat. It even tasted pretty good. I ate almost all of it.

"That was good," I said, meaning it.

Marcia looked pleased. "I know you don't want to talk, but we could play a game. I could tell you about school yesterday," she said.

We played a couple of games. I didn't realize what a good time I was having until she stood and put on her coat. "I have to leave now if I'm going to take

Sam for a walk. My mom's coming in a few minutes."

She started for the door again and then suddenly ran back and kissed me quickly on the cheek.

I stared after her and touched my cheek. There was a snicker from the kitchen doorway. "Oh, Martin. You are sooo wonderful," Caroline said.

"You were spying on me," I whispered loudly.

"I couldn't resist," Caroline said. She clasped her hands over her heart. "Martin and Marcia, sitting in a tree, k-i-s-s-i-n-g," she chanted.

I threw my pillow at her.

"Touchy, touchy. I guess love does that to you." Caroline laughed as she ducked around the doorway.

15

Tempers and Toenails

MARCIA STOPPED BY for the next two days to take Sam for a walk. Afterward she would stay and visit. Caroline watched us like a hawk, but Marcia didn't try to kiss me again. By Tuesday I was ready to go back to school and Marcia had beaten me in twelve games of cards, two games of Scrabble, and one game of Monopoly.

Almost all of the relatives had responded to the invitations, and most of them were coming. Mom nervously read the long-range weather forecasts, but it looked as if even Mother Nature was cooperating with the reunion plans. Spring was in the air. Flowers were popping up, and the trees were in leaf.

The next few weeks Aunt Henrietta trained even

harder. Sometimes I ran with her, but I could never last as long as she did. Usually I would have to stop and rest until she caught up with me on the way back. Actually, I kind of enjoyed the running. With all that practice, I had even come in second when we'd run laps around the gym at school.

On the last Saturday in March, Willie was eating dinner with us. He took a bite of lasagna and rolled his eyes with delight. "Mrs. Albright, you are such a good cook."

Mrs. Albright beamed at him. "Save some room for the strawberry pie I made for dessert."

"Don't worry," Willie assured her.

"I have to go potty," Robbie announced. He jumped down from his chair. "I'll be right back," he said.

"It's not fair," Caroline said, picking at her own dinner. "Willie and Tim eat like horses and both of them are skinny."

"That's because both of them are growing so fast," Dad said.

I cast an envious look at Willie. He had grown a lot this year. The shirt he'd gotten for Christmas was already too short to cover his wrists.

"I wish I'd grow," I said.

"Don't worry," Mom said. "One of these days you'll just start shooting up."

"I wish I'd stop growing," Caroline said. "All my

114

friends are skinny. I'm just a blob." She put down her fork.

"Going without eating is not a good way to lose weight," Dad said gently. "And anyway, you are at a perfectly healthy weight."

"Plump," Tim mouthed around another bite of lasagna. "That's a good word. Pl . . . ump."

"That's enough," Dad said sternly.

"Be glad that you have all this good food," Aunt Henrietta began. "Children in the countries where I've taught—"

"I don't want to hear about other countries. And I don't want to hear about being healthy," Caroline raged. She stood up and pushed back her chair so hard it almost tipped over. "I don't want to be healthy. I want to be beautiful." She ran out of the room.

There was a moment of stunned silence at the table.

Tim calmly stuffed another bite of lasagna in his mouth.

"I'll go talk to her," Mom said.

Aunt Henrietta looked stricken. "I feel so awful. Caroline wanted to hear that she was pretty, and instead I start telling her about starving children."

"Caroline is just going through a stage," Dad said.

"Caroline's whole life is a stage," Tim said.

Dad held up his hand. "Do I hear water running?"

From the downstairs bathroom we heard a small voice. "I flushed," Robbie called.

Everyone ran to the bathroom. Already water was pouring out into the hall from the clogged toilet. "Robbie," Dad said grimly, "what did you flush down the toilet?"

Robbie hung his head. "Car."

"Robbie's going through a flushing stage," Tim said.

"Never ever flush again!" Dad roared.

"I'll call the plumber," Mom said as she came downstairs and saw the mess.

"You are lucky to live in a big family," Willie said later after the plumber had done his work and gone. We were out in the yard tossing a ball for Sam to catch. "There's always something going on at your house."

I shook my head. "Sometimes I wish I was an only child."

Willie rolled on the grass with Sam. "It's boring, believe me."

"I think I'd like to be bored. It's like a zoo around here sometimes. And it's going to be even worse when all these relatives come. What if Robbie flushes something down the toilet then?"

Willie shrugged and grinned. "I guess your dad will call the plumber."

After Willie left, I went back inside. The whole family was sitting in the living room talking about the reunion. Caroline was there, too, although she still looked unhappy.

"I just hope the weather is nice," Mom said.

"Since the reunion is on Easter weekend, we should have an Easter egg hunt," I suggested.

"Good idea," Mom said. "That would be a nice project for you."

"I could help you," Caroline offered. "We could mark some of the eggs and have prizes."

Aunt Henrietta sat on the couch and kicked off her shoes. She rubbed her big toe.

"You haven't gone running for three days," I said. "You might get out of shape."

"I hurt my toe a couple of days ago," she answered ruefully.

Her toe was purple and swollen, and the toenail looked strange.

"Gross," Caroline whispered.

"Let me see," Dad said. "How in the world did you do this?"

"One of the workmen at the new post office was walking by with a stack of bricks. The top one slipped off and landed right on my toe."

"That looks pretty bad," Dad said. "Better come in the office, and I'll tend it for you."

Aunt Henrietta hobbled after him.

"What if she can't be in the race after all this work?" I said.

"I have a feeling it will take more than a smashed toe to stop Aunt Henrietta," said Mom.

After a while Dad and Aunt Henrietta came out of his office. There was a bandage on Aunt Henrietta's big toe. "Well, it's not broken," Dad said. "But she's going to lose the nail, I think, and it's badly bruised."

"All this fuss about a toe," Caroline whispered under her breath.

"I had an ingrown toenail once," Tim said. "It got infected and it really hurt."

"You probably got the infection from those smelly shoes you wear." Caroline sneered.

"I'd rather have stinky feet than stinky breath like you," Tim retorted.

Robbie zoomed his cars around the living room floor. "Stinky, stinky, stinky," he chanted.

I thought about Willie going home to his nice quiet house. Some people just don't know when they are lucky.

16

Water Balloons and a Pen

EASTER WEEKEND FINALLY arrived. There wasn't any school on Friday. A lot of the out-of-town visitors were arriving, and we all had to help with the last-minute preparations. Tim and I were still picking up branches that had fallen during the winter, and then we had to rake the yard.

"How am I going to play baseball if my hands are all blistered," Tim complained to Dad.

Dad was up on a ladder cleaning leaves (and making more raking for us) out of the rain gutters on the porch roof. He climbed down and walked around inspecting everything. I thought the place looked pretty good. It seemed to me it was silly to clean so much before the relatives came. I mean, with all

119

those people tramping around, it was not going to stay clean for long.

Dad finished his inspection tour and nodded. "You boys did a good job."

"You mean we can go?" Tim said hopefully.

"Not yet," Dad said. "We need to set up the tent."

We dragged the tent out of the garage and started pounding in the stakes in a shady spot at the side of the house. The tent had a faint musty odor. The last time we'd gone camping, Dad had gotten sprayed by a skunk.

Mom called us in for lunch just as we finished. "I want to get the dishes done before anyone comes," she said.

After lunch, Willie rode by on his bike. Some men were just delivering the picnic tables Mom had rented for the weekend. Aunt Henrietta dragged three new garbage cans from the garage. With everyone eating off paper plates all weekend, there was bound to be a lot of trash.

I noticed she was still limping slightly. All day she had been charging around like a human dynamo. I wondered if she was going to change before people arrived. Right now she was wearing neon-orange baggy shorts and purple bedroom slippers.

"Boy. Your family thought of everything," Willie said. "My grandma would be in a panic by now."

"Don't worry," I said. "Mom's in the kitchen pac-

ing up and down, trying to think if she forgot anything."

Willie waved good-bye. "Have fun," he shouted as
he pedaled away. I sat down to rest near our tent.

Some of the relatives weren't coming until Saturday, but a few were staying for the entire weekend.
Even though Mom was still worried, I thought we
were ready for them. The house was scrubbed from
top to bottom, and the refrigerator and cupboards
were stocked with more food than I'd ever seen any-
where except in the grocery store.

Tim got a bag of chips from the kitchen and hid
it in the tent along with an extra flashlight and some
games. Tim, Caroline, and I were sleeping in the tent
so Grandma and Grandpa and Great-Grandpa Snodgrass could stay in the house.

They were the first to arrive. After lunch, Dad had
driven to the airport and picked them up. Grandma
and Grandpa Snodgrass live in Florida, so we don't
see them very often. Grandpa's hair is still mostly
red. He doesn't hear very well, so he talks pretty loud,
mainly about golf. The first thing he did was measure
us to see how much we'd all grown. "You children
are certainly growing fast," he said. "Next thing you
know, you will all be grown-up." He winked at
Grandma. "We must be getting old to have grand-
children this big."

Grandma sniffed. "Maybe you are, but I'm not,"

she said. She pushed her blond curls back in place after hugging Aunt Henrietta.

Great-Grandpa didn't say much. He just sat in Dad's favorite chair.

Robbie patted his face. "Why is your face so bumpy?" he asked.

Great-Grandpa chuckled. "Those are wrinkles. I have them because I'm so smart."

Robbie patted his own face. "I wish I had wrinkles," he said.

"Who are you?" Great-Grandpa asked Tim.

"This is Tim and Caroline and Martin," Aunt Henrietta told him. "They are your great-grandchildren."

"Grandpa is getting a little forgetful," Grandma said.

"I have a present for you," Great-Grandpa told Tim. He reached in his pocket and handed him a pen.

"Thanks," Tim said. "I really don't need it, though."

"No, no," Great-Grandpa insisted. "It's a present."

Tim looked a little uncomfortable still, but he put the pen in his shirt pocket and sat down.

Robbie seemed fascinated with Great-Grandpa's wrinkles. He leaned over the chair studying Great-Grandpa's face.

"Who is this boy?" Great-Grandpa asked.

"This is Robbie," Grandma told him.

Great-Grandpa held Robbie on his lap and admired

Robbie's cars. Suddenly he looked up at Tim. "Say, that's a nice pen I see sticking out of your pocket. Would you mind if I borrowed it?"

Tim handed it back. Great-Grandpa looked at it and then stuck it back in his pocket.

Other relatives were arriving. Aunt Jane and Uncle Dave had brought their own tent and pitched it next to ours. "It sure is hot," Uncle Dave said, pausing to wipe his forehead.

"The weatherman says this is the hottest spring Ohio has had for fifty years," Tim said.

Our Ohio cousins, Matt, Tabitha, and Corey, grinned at us. We knew them pretty well. With their red hair and freckles, they looked enough like us to be brothers and sisters.

"This is going to be fun," Matt said. He was the closest to my age.

"Tomorrow, when everyone is here, we'll play baseball," Tim said, with a look at me. He knows I'm not very good at sports.

"Just be sure to do it in the backyard," Dad said. "That way any stray balls will go in the field and not in someone's lap."

"You are lucky to have such a big yard," Corey said. "If the reunion had been at our house, no one would have been able to move."

"What shall we do?" Tabitha asked.

"I've got an idea," Matt said. He reached in his bag

with a mischievous look and pulled out a bag of balloons. "How about a water balloon fight?"

While we were talking, a car pulled in the driveway. I recognized two cousins from California from the pictures Aunt Henrietta had showed me. I had never met them before. Their family was staying at one of the motels in town. They were teenagers and had great suntans and weird clothes. They sort of sneered at us when we ran over and asked if they wanted to join us.

"Get real," the girl said in a bored voice.

We snuck around to the spigot at the back of the house to fill up the balloons.

The grown-ups were all gathered around the picnic tables, talking. We looked for our unfriendly cousins, but they had disappeared.

We stood around with our full balloons. Caroline seemed to know what I was thinking. "If we dump these balloons on them, we'll get in trouble," she warned.

"Not if it is an accident." Matt grinned. "They might walk right into where we are playing."

I was the one who spotted them. They were hiding behind the garage.

"They're smoking!" Caroline exclaimed.

Tim grinned. "We'd better put out the fire before they hurt themselves."

Running around the corner of the garage, we

yelled, "Catch!" and threw the balloons.

"You rotten little jerks," the girl screamed. Water streamed down her face, and her carefully combed hair hung in wet straggles.

After the first angry look, the boy laughed, but our other cousin was still unhappy. "I'm going to tell," she said, sounding exactly like Caroline.

"Oh, come on, Andrea, they were just playing," the boy said.

"You'll probably want to explain about the cigarettes, too," Tabitha said.

Andrea glared. "You little dweebs. I knew I'd hate this family reunion."

Laughing, we ran back to the picnic tables. Some of the uncles were playing horseshoes, and Mrs. Albright was bringing out a big platter of lunch meats and rolls to make sandwiches. Grandma, Mom, and Dad followed with chips and a plate of vegetables for dipping. It was cooling off a little, and it was almost dark.

Great-Grandpa came out of the house. "You look like a nice young man," he said to Uncle Dave. "I've got something for you." He reached in his pocket and handed the pen to Uncle Dave.

The two teens filled their plates. The boy winked as he passed, and I decided he wasn't so bad after all. The girl stood next to a woman who was an older version of herself. The woman looked bored and picked at her food when her husband brought her a plate.

"I hope we don't have very many relatives like them," I told Tim.

Robbie was playing trucks with a little boy named Tommie. Mom and Tommie's mother took them into the house to wash their hands. Both of the boys were screaming at the top of their lungs, not wanting to stop playing.

Caroline shook her head. "What's it going to be like tomorrow when the rest of the relatives arrive?"

Great-Grandpa took his plate and wobbled over to Uncle Dave. "Say," he said, "that's a nice pen. I used to have one just like it."

"Would you like it?" Uncle Dave asked, handing it to him.

Great-Grandpa smiled broadly. Then he tucked the pen in his pocket and sat back down with his meal.

17

Even More Relatives

ON SATURDAY WE were up early. I hadn't slept very well crowded in the tent with Tim and Caroline, and it was already sticky and hot.

Caroline glanced at the thermometer that hung by the back door. "It's already eighty degrees outside. I've never seen it this hot in April."

"Mom was worried about snow, remember?" Tim remarked.

We stumbled into the house and found a line waiting for the bathrooms. Grandpa was in Mom and Dad's bathroom taking a shower, and Aunt Jane and Uncle Dave were in the main bathroom.

"Oh, great," Caroline said sourly. "We get to wait in line for our own bathroom."

"It's only for one day," Mom said. "And I'm sure it will only be for a few minutes."

The few minutes turned into nearly an hour, and by the time I got my turn there wasn't any hot water left. Everyone was in a pretty good mood, though. Caroline cheered up when she finally got her turn, and after breakfast she even offered to help me color the eggs for the Easter egg hunt. Mom helped us boil six dozen eggs. When they had boiled for ten minutes, we let them sit for a few minutes in cold water.

We covered the table with newspapers and dropped little tablets of color into cupfuls of water. Matt, Tabitha, and Corey arrived to help.

Dad left to go to the hospital to check on his patients. Even though he had arranged not to have any appointments all weekend, he had to visit the patients who were already sick. Mom went to the motels to pick up people who hadn't rented cars. Several more families who lived close enough to drive were arriving today.

We took turns using the dye until all the eggs were colored. "How are we going to mark the prize eggs?" I asked. We had a few prizes for the winner and runners-up.

"How about numbers?" Caroline suggested. She took a marker, drew a star, and put a number 1 inside.

"My mom hid eggs in the house last Easter because it was raining. We didn't find one of them for three weeks." Corey held his nose. "Phew!"

"We'd better hurry if we are going to have these hidden before everyone gets here," Tim said. He drew the number 2 on another egg.

We put the eggs back in the egg boxes to dry and dumped the cups in the sink. Caroline rolled up the newspapers and put them in the trash.

We fanned out to hide the eggs. Since everyone was gathering in the front yard we hid the eggs around the back of the house. We put some in easy sight for the really little kids. Others we hid in bushes and trees. Uncle George was pounding in stakes for a horseshoe game off to one side of the backyard, and Grandpa and Aunt Judith were putting up the volleyball net. "Don't let anyone over here," Caroline said with a sweeping gesture. "They might step on some eggs."

Mom was just returning with the first load of relatives when we finished.

The kitchen was rapidly filling up with food. All the relatives who lived nearby had brought covered dishes for lunch. The refrigerator was filled with interesting and good-smelling things to eat.

"Did you get the eggs all hidden?" Mom asked as she tucked still another casserole in the refrigerator.

"All done," I answered.

Mom looked out the window with a worried glance. "We had better do it soon. The Weather Channel is predicting thunderstorms late this afternoon."

"What will we do with all these people if it storms?" Caroline asked.

"Crowd them in the house, I guess," Mom said. "Let's hope the storm will be a quick one." Ohio often has ferocious thunderstorms during periods of unusually hot weather. But they usually last only ten or fifteen minutes.

I wandered around the yard. Everyone was kissing and hugging. I knew most of them, but it was the first time I had seen so many members of my family all together. It was amazing to think I was related to all these people. Everyone seemed especially glad to see Aunt Henrietta, and she was floating with happiness. All morning she walked around hugging and smiling and mixing up everyone's names. I was kind of glad the tape hadn't driven her away and made her miss this day.

Mom announced the egg hunt, and everyone moved to the backyard to watch. Grandpa stood on a chair. "Let's give the youngest children a few seconds' head start," he said. There were about ten kids under five lined up at the house. "On your mark, get set, go!" he shouted.

The older kids lined up, too, but Grandpa made them wait. Some of the little children didn't know what to do, and their moms and dads were pointing to the eggs. After a minute, Grandpa let the rest of the kids go. They swarmed across the yard. In less than a minute it was all over.

Caroline shook her head. "It took us two hours to do all those eggs."

I got to pass out the prizes. First prize was a big stuffed bunny. A little girl with bright red curls won it. Her name was Lisa, and she was a second cousin from New York I'd never met before. She sat right down on the grass and hugged and petted the bunny as though it were alive.

Aunt Henrietta stood by beaming at me. She had on a big straw hat to keep out the sun. "Isn't this wonderful," she exclaimed. "You are part of all this."

I thought about the family tree Miss Lawson had given me. I wouldn't even know where to put everyone. Maybe instead of branches they'd have to be little leaves. It made me smile, thinking of turning each person into a leaf. Maybe all the young ones would be buds, just starting to open. And Great-Grandpa would be an old leaf, curled and wrinkled, blowing in the wind.

I kept picturing everyone that way as I wandered around, listening to the conversations. Great-Grandpa was making his way through the crowd, passing out his pen and collecting it back again.

I saw Andrea. She was sitting under a tree polishing her fingernails bright red. She glared at me as I walked by. I thought about her being a little fungus growing on that family tree and it made me smile.

At noon the picnic tables were filled with every kind of food you could imagine. Even though I only took a tiny bit of each thing, my plate was heaping. I took my plate and sat down under a tree. Caroline joined me.

"Amazing, isn't it?" she said, waving her arms at the crowd.

"I can't even remember half their names," I admitted.

"I did meet one girl I liked. We figured out she's a second cousin. She's just like me. She's going to a special school for gifted kids. We're going to be pen pals."

After lunch, Tim organized a softball game. A lot of people wandered to the backyard to watch.

Mom walked by holding a tired-looking Robbie. "I'm going to see if I can get him to take a nap," she said.

"No nap," Robbie whispered in a sleepy voice.

Several other parents took the youngest children inside the house to rest. I let Sam out of the garage for some exercise.

"Is that your dog?" Andrea was leaning against a tree watching.

I nodded.

"He's cute," Andrea said, bending down to pat Sam.

"He knows how to shake hands," I bragged. "Shake, Sam." I held out my hand.

Sam put his paw in my hand.

"Can he do anything else?" asked Andrea.

"Not yet," I said. "I haven't had him very long."

"My mom wouldn't let me have a dog. She doesn't like animals."

Sam rolled over and let her scratch his tummy. "I didn't want to come here," Andrea said. She smiled a little. "I guess you could tell, huh?" She sighed. "All my friends wanted me to do stuff with them on Easter vacation. And here I am with a bunch of people I don't even know. I mean, who cares? We will probably never see each other again, right?"

I nodded. "Where is your brother?"

"Jason? Oh, he's playing softball. He's having a good time. He likes your brother Tim."

Aunt Henrietta came outside wearing her running shoes. "I ate too much lunch," she confided. "I think I'll take a little run. Do you feel like escaping the crowds for a while, or are you enjoying yourself?"

"It's pretty warm," I said.

"I'm not going to go very far—or very fast," she added. "My toe is a little sore."

Sam jumped eagerly around us. I knew he would like to have a chance to explore. I snapped on his leash, and we set off down the road at a leisurely pace.

Aunt Henrietta was running awkwardly, keeping her foot with the injured toe flat. We passed the cornfield and turned down a gravel road. The air was still and heavy, and sweat made my back itch.

"I guess you were right," Aunt Henrietta admitted. "It *is* too hot to run. Let's rest a minute."

We sat on a large boulder by the side of the road. Sam plopped beside us, his tongue hanging out as he panted.

Aunt Henrietta looked up at the sky. "It seems a funny color, don't you think?"

"Mom said she heard there might be thunderstorms this afternoon," I said.

"Maybe we'd just better head back," Aunt Henrietta said. She stood up, then suddenly grabbed my arm. "What's that?"

I listened. From the direction of town I could hear the wail of a siren. "That's the tornado siren," I yelled. "Come on!"

We sprinted toward home. The sky was getting a purplish tint and growing darker. "Come on," urged Aunt Henrietta. "That siren is so far away that they may not have heard it, especially with everyone talking. Let's cut across the field."

We left the road and started across the field. To save time we ran diagonally, but it was harder to run across the freshly plowed furrows. Aunt Henrietta was running slightly ahead of me, but suddenly Sam bounded right in front of her feet and she went sprawling.

I tried to help her up. "Are you all right?" I shouted anxiously.

She grabbed her ankle. "I may have sprained it."

"See if you can run," I said. I cast a nervous look at the sky. It was an unfriendly shade of purple.

Aunt Henrietta took a few wobbly steps. "You'd better leave me here. You can send back help."

"No, I can't do that," I said with a worried look at the sky. A flash of lightning zigzagged to the ground not far away. "Lean on me," I said. "We'll make it." She steadied herself against me. I could tell she was in pain, but she kept on going. If I hadn't been so scared, it might have looked funny. We probably looked like runners in a three-legged race.

Aunt Henrietta's face was pale. "Come on," I encouraged her. "We're almost there."

The wind was getting stronger now. I could see the baseball players through the trees that separated our yard from the field. Some people who had been sitting and watching the game were standing up, looking around with growing alarm.

"Help!" I screamed. The wind seemed to blow my words away before I was heard.

At last people seemed to notice. They were pointing at us, and Uncle Dave and Dad were running to help.

"Go back," Aunt Henrietta shouted.

Suddenly I was aware of a sound. A roaring noise, far away but coming closer. I looked behind me just as the men reached us. Far away I saw a huge black cloud that grew smaller closer to the ground. The cloud was angry, swirling, coming closer even as I watched.

"Tornado!" I screamed. "It's heading right for us."

18

Tornado

IT SEEMED AS if things were happening in slow motion, although everyone was moving fast. Dad and Uncle Dave reached us just as I thought my legs would give out. "Run for the house!" Dad yelled as he reached out a hand to steady me. He and Uncle Dave almost carried Aunt Henrietta. The wind was blowing harder now, bending the trees with its force.

I reached the yard. Mom was at the door. "Everyone get inside," she screamed.

The wind was swirling little pieces of dirt and twigs that stung when they hit your skin. Uncle George and Grandpa were leading Great-Grandpa into the house. I saw Lisa, the little girl with her prize rabbit. She was standing by the garage staring at the rapidly approaching funnel as though she was too frightened to move. I scooped her up as I raced for the door.

The roar was louder now. People were crowding down the stairs to the basement. The little girl's mother was there, holding a small baby. "Oh, thank you, thank you," she cried. With the little girl in one arm and the baby in the other, she started down the stairs.

"Sam," I yelled. "I forgot Sam."

Andrea burst through the door carrying Sam like a baby. "I've got him."

Dad and Uncle Dave reached the house, and willing hands helped Aunt Henrietta down the stairs. "We need to open a couple of windows," Dad shouted to Uncle Dave. I remembered that I'd heard that in school. Opening windows relieved some of the air pressure in the house. I ran to help Dad open the dining room window. Uncle Dave opened a window on the other side of the house.

"Get downstairs," Dad yelled at me over the roar.

"Is everyone in?" Uncle Dave was yelling, too.

"Yes." Through the window Dad had just opened I could see the funnel. It was ugly and black, but it skipped along like a ballerina lightly tiptoeing across a stage. When it touched the earth, whole trees were wrenched from the ground and thrown down as though they were twigs. It was like looking inside some sort of giant vacuum cleaner gone crazy. I was nearly paralyzed with fear.

Dad grabbed my arm and almost dragged me to

the basement door just as the last few people made it down the narrow stairs. I saw Andrea just ahead of me. She was still holding on to Sam. Dad and Uncle Dave came right after me, closing the door behind them.

The roar was slightly less. Everyone was crowded into the unfinished room that Dad had been trying to turn into an extra family room for years. Several men had taken pieces of paneling and were nailing them over the windows.

Some of the children were crying, and their mothers were trying to calm them down.

"We're going to be all right," came Aunt Henrietta's calm voice. "This is one family reunion no one will forget."

"That's for sure," Uncle George said with a chuckle.

Suddenly the lights went out. Someone screamed. "I'm scared, Martin," Robbie said.

"We'll be okay," I called out. But I wasn't feeling too confident. The house seemed to creak and moan, and sometimes we could hear a loud bang as though something had crashed against the wall. I was frozen in terror. I heard a soft whine, and a furry body wriggled next to me. I put my arms around Sam. He was trembling, but he licked my nose to comfort me.

Aunt Henrietta's voice rose over the storm. "She'll be coming round the mountain," she sang. Her voice was clear and strong. After a minute other voices joined in.

There was a crash and a tinkle of glass from the laundry room as a window blew in. Now we could hear the storm again in all its fury. My ears felt funny.

"I don't like this dark," I heard a little girl say from across the room.

"There's an emergency flashlight plugged in along the wall," Dad said.

"Found it," Matt shouted, and the room was suddenly lit with enough light for us to see one another's frightened faces.

"It sounds as if the storm is moving off," Dad said. "But we'd better stay here a few more minutes to make sure it doesn't change direction. Is everybody all right?"

"I skinned my knee," Tim said.

"You did that playing baseball," Caroline said.

"It sounds better to say it was the tornado," Tim said.

"I'll go up and look around," Dad said at last.

He and Uncle Dave disappeared up the steps. A few minutes later, Uncle Dave called back down, "It's still storming, but the worst seems to be over."

People lined up to climb the stairs. I was surprised to find that the kitchen looked almost normal. But the living room was a disaster. A large tree branch had crashed through the picture window. Glass, leaves, and dirt had blown everywhere.

Uncle George had stepped outside. "Wow"—he tried to joke—"it looks like a tornado came through here."

The storm had done strange things as it skipped along. The picnic tables were still in place, but I could see one of the benches across the street. A car in the driveway was tipped over on its side, and the mailbox was gone. The whole top of a maple tree was gone, or maybe that was what had come through the front window. The yard was littered with little squares of something. "Roofing tiles," Dad said.

The new outdoor grill seemed to have disappeared along with all the baseballs, bats, and gloves dropped in the panic.

But the storm had not just taken things. It had left us some presents, too. The yard was full of papers, pieces of boards, and even an old lawn chair I'd never seen before.

Mrs. Albright pushed anxiously by me. "I've got to check on Harold," she called. But just then Mr. DeWitt's door opened. He stepped out on his porch and waved. Mrs. Albright ran over and they hugged.

Dad went back in to check the phones, but they were dead. "I'd better drive to town and see if anyone was hurt," Dad said.

Mom was still holding Robbie. She looked pale and stricken as she stared at the mess in the living room.

Aunt Henrietta put her arm around Mom's shoulders. "I think we were pretty lucky," Aunt Henrietta remarked. "No one was hurt, and with all these people here we will have this mess cleaned up in no time. It takes more than a little tornado to wipe out the Snodgrass family."

Almost like magic, work was divided. Andrea and several of the older girls took charge of the small children. Some of us scoured the yard, picking up the trash and small branches. Several of the aunts swept up the glass from the front room while the uncles got out chain saws to cut up the fallen trees. By the time the electricity came on that evening, the house, except for the missing window, looked almost normal.

Dad returned and reported that the storm had bypassed the town. "It knocked down two barns and demolished a trailer, but no one was hurt except for a man who was hit by a tree branch flying through the air," he said. "He just needed a couple of stitches on his head."

The man from the glass shop arrived. He covered the window with plastic and promised to replace the glass the next day. The garage came and towed away the overturned car.

"I'm hungry," Grandpa announced.

"Pizza," someone suggested.

"I'd like to see the pizza guy's face when we call

up and order enough pizza for seventy people," Tim whispered.

In the end Dad ordered pizza from three different pizza shops. The delivery boys did look amazed when they saw the crowd that was waiting for them. Everyone seemed different somehow, as though the afternoon had bound us together. A family, I suddenly realized. As the stars came out, people drifted away. Some were heading back to the motels and would return on Sunday, but a few were heading home. I was sorry to see each one go—even Andrea and her brother.

"Thanks for saving Sam," I said.

Andrea shrugged. "I like dogs." She smiled. "I thought I would hate it here, but it was kind of nice. And I doubt if any of my friends can say they lived through a tornado."

"If you come to California someday, we'll show you around," her brother said.

"Maybe we can arrange an earthquake if you get bored," Andrea joked.

Great-Grandpa walked by. "I've got something for you," he said, handing me the pen.

"Thank you," I said. "It's very nice."

I waved good-bye to several more departing relatives and then went to hunt up Great-Grandpa. He was sitting on the lawn chair the tornado had given us.

"Here's your pen, Grandpa," I said, holding it out to him.

Great-Grandpa winked slowly and patted my hand. "Oh no, son. I gave it to you."

19

Martin the Hero

"DAD, WILL YOU tell Robbie he can flush again?" Caroline said at breakfast a few days later. "It's embarrassing. What if one of my friends should use the bathroom after Robbie?"

I looked at Robbie, who was running a piece of French toast over his high-chair tray like a car.

"Maybe when he's twenty I'll let him flush again," Dad said from behind the morning paper.

Caroline sighed, but she didn't grouch anymore. Maybe she was happy because Mom had finally allowed her to wear lipstick to school. It was not very dark and you could hardly see it, but Caroline kept touching her lips as though she wanted to make sure it was still there.

"I've been invited to computer camp at the college this summer," she announced. "My teacher said we will stay in the dorms. There were only two kids picked in the whole town."

Dad put down the paper. "That's wonderful."

"I think I'll be going somewhere this summer, too," Tim bragged. "My coach said he thinks I'll be picked for the Baseball All-Stars. That means I'll get to travel around playing other state teams."

"I'm really proud of you children," Mom said.

"I'm not doing anything special," I mumbled.

"But you are our hero," Mom said.

I paused with a forkful of French toast halfway to my mouth. "What do you mean?"

"You saved Aunt Henrietta and that little girl, dummy," Tim said. "And maybe the rest of us, too. If we'd noticed just a minute later, someone might have been hurt."

I grinned. "I never thought about it. I guess I was a hero."

"Don't let it go to your head," Caroline teased. "You're still a dweeb."

"Lisa and her mother were staying for a week with friends in New Albany," Mom said. "One of them is a reporter for the *New Albany Sentinel*. He wants to do an article about you in the paper tomorrow. As a matter of fact, he wants to come and take a picture of you this afternoon."

Tim pounded me on the back. "Way to go!" he yelled. "My brother the hero."

Caroline laughed. "Remember last year when you were trying to think of some way to be famous?"

I felt my face getting red. I hadn't realized she knew about that. Once I had even chased a cat up a tree so I could rescue it and get my picture in the paper.

"I'm not sure I'm a hero," I admitted. "I was so scared my knees were shaking."

"That makes you all the braver," Aunt Henrietta said warmly. "You did it all in spite of your fear."

That afternoon Lisa and her mother came to the house. Lisa's mom was one of Dad's cousins. The reporter wanted us all there so he could take a picture of us together. Lisa was still holding the bunny, and she leaned over and gave me a kiss just as the photographer snapped a picture.

It was on the front page of the newspaper the next morning. The headline said: *A Kiss for a Hero,* and there was a big article that made me sound braver than I really was.

Dad went out and bought a whole stack of papers so he could send the article to all our relatives. The phone rang all night long with people calling to congratulate me.

When I got off the school bus the next morning, everyone clapped. Mr. Higgenbottom patted me on the back and told me he was proud of me.

"That was a really brave thing you did," Marcia said at recess.

"It really wasn't that much," I said. "I thought it would be really great to get all this attention, but it's kind of embarrassing."

"Well, I think you are very brave," she said. "And you are the nicest boy I know."

"He's the tornado kid," Willie said. "He comes swooping down, saving fair maidens in distress." He slouched against the school wall. "You're lucky. The storm didn't come close to my house."

"You're the one that's lucky," I said. "I never want to see a storm like that again."

"I would have been scared," Willie said.

"I was," I told him. "When we were all down in the basement, I was afraid our whole house was going to blow away. I've never been so scared in all my life."

Willie reached over and rubbed my head with his knuckles. "Of course you were," he said, in a perfect imitation of Aunt Henrietta.

I wiggled away from Willie's head rub and grinned at him. Willie was the type of friend you could tell anything to and he would understand.

"Someday I'm going to write a story about you," he said. "And then when I'm a famous actor, maybe they'll make it into a movie."

"Who would play me?" I asked.

Willie pretended to think. Then he gave me a knowing smile. "How about 'Cousin Agnes'?" he suggested slyly.

20

Another Surprise

MOM HAD ANOTHER surprise for me. "How would you like to go to Boston and watch the race?" she asked at breakfast. "Aunt Henrietta would like you to come."

"That would be great," I exclaimed. "But is she going to be able to run?"

"She's determined to try," Mom said. "Fortunately, it wasn't a bad sprain."

"I have an old friend living in Boston," Mrs. Albright said. She put a plate stacked high with golden brown pancakes on the table. "Her name is Deborah Sims. Since her children have grown and moved away she is all alone in her great big old house. She said she would love some company."

I speared three pancakes and reached for the syrup. "What about school?" I asked.

"I already talked to Miss Lawson," Mom said. "She thinks it will be a good educational experience."

"Do Tim and I get to go, too?" asked Caroline. She frowned at the five pancakes on Tim's plate and put one on her own.

"Not this time," Mom said. "Martin is the one who has gone running almost every time with Aunt Henrietta. Both of you have some exciting things coming up, and I think Martin has earned this trip. I'm going, too. The three of us will fly there early Sunday morning. Mrs. Albright's friend is picking us up at the airport."

"The race actually starts in a little town called Hopkinton," Aunt Henrietta said later. "We will run a little over twenty-six miles into Boston."

"That's a long ways," I said.

"At least the weather is a lot cooler," she said. After the tornado the temperature had dropped to a more normal sixty-five degrees. "And the television says it's about the same in Boston. I'm not sure I would have made it if it had remained hot."

After breakfast on Saturday morning, Aunt Henrietta put on her running shoes. Dad had showed her how to wrap her ankle for extra support. "This will be my last run before the big race," she announced. "Anyone want to join me?" Caroline hid behind the book on Greek history she was reading and pretended not to hear.

"I've got baseball practice in a few minutes," Tim said.

"I'll go," I said. I slipped into the running shoes Mom and Dad had bought me way back in February.

We did a few stretching exercises on the front porch. "Miss Lawson says the race is always on Patriots' Day," I told her. "That's the third Monday in April. She told us that last year there were nine thousand runners."

We started off at a smooth pace. "I won't be coming back after the race," she said. "I'm returning to my work."

I stopped running. "Why? I thought you liked it here."

Aunt Henrietta ran in place while she talked. "I do. It's been a wonderful visit. But it's good to go where I am really needed. The director of a refugee camp called last week. He's an old colleague of mine. He asked me to start a school for the children. It will be a real challenge because there isn't much money to use for schooling. Or anything else, for that matter."

"That sounds hard," I said.

"It is hard," Aunt Henrietta said. "It is also wonderful. I love what I do. I thought I wanted to retire a few months ago. But I really just needed a break, a time to get to know my family."

I wondered what Aunt Henrietta's new students would think of her. Would they see only a lady with bony knees and wild hair? I hoped it wouldn't take them as long as it had taken me to see the really great person underneath.

We started running again. I noticed a little limp and knew that her foot was still hurting. "Aunt Henrietta," I said, panting, "I never understood why this race is so important to you."

When she answered, her voice was steady and strong in spite of the distance we'd run. "When I was young, I was a pretty good athlete. In fact, I even dreamed of the Olympics. But there were no long-distance races for women back then, and I could never compete as a sprinter. Then I visited a friend who was working in an orphanage run by our church. Before I knew it, I was working there, too."

I nodded to show I understood. "So you never got a chance to do what you really wanted?"

"No, I didn't mean that. I did do what I wanted with my life. I did, however, always wonder if I could have made the Olympics, especially when women began to compete in longer races." She smiled. "I'm a little old for the Olympics now. Actually, I hadn't thought of running in the marathon until I read an article about it just before I flew home. I've kept in pretty good shape, and I just decided I wanted to try." Her voice was serious, as if she were talking to a grown-up.

"I think you'll make it," I said.

"Thank you." She glanced over at me. "I'm glad we had time to become friends. I know living with an old lady can be a pain sometimes."

I stopped for a minute to catch my breath. "I will be glad to get my room back. Sleeping in a room with Tim's sneakers—now, *that's* a pain."

We packed the car for the trip to the airport that night. Aunt Henrietta played with Robbie, chasing him around while they both barked like dogs.

"It will be nice to get back like we were. No more family stories, no more tales of starving kids," Caroline said as she watched Aunt Henrietta and Robbie. Then she smiled. "It's hard to believe, but I think I'm going to miss Aunt Henrietta."

"Me too," Tim said.

"How do you think she's going to do in the race?" Caroline asked.

Tim shook his head. "She's pretty stubborn. And she is a good runner, but I don't think she'll make it."

"She will," I said. I glared at Tim.

"She's sixty years old," Caroline said. "And I think her ankle still hurts. Tim's right. She won't make it. But it is kind of neat that she's trying."

21

Another Kind of Brave

THE PLANE TO Boston was packed. I had never flown before, so I was pretty excited. After we took off, the flight attendant came around and gave me some juice. By the time I drank it, the plane was starting to land. Only a little more than an hour ago we had been in Columbus.

Mrs. Albright's friend, Mrs. Sims, was at the Boston airport, holding a sign with our name. She whisked us away to her house, pointing out some of the sights along the way. "Too bad you are not going to be here longer," she said. "Boston is full of history. I could show you Paul Revere's house and the site of the Boston Massacre."

We pulled up in front of a brick house. It almost

157

touched the houses on either side of it. All the houses on the narrow street looked almost the same. Inside, it was cozy and comfortable, with big soft chairs and couches and a furry rug in front of a huge fireplace in the front room. Mrs. Sims led us up a narrow staircase and opened the first door. "This was my son's room," she said. "He's away at college."

It was small but nice. Several airplane models hung from wire hooked to the ceiling. "This will be great," I said.

Mrs. Sims fixed some fancy sandwiches and soup for lunch. The ladies stayed at the table talking after we ate. I excused myself and went outside to sit on the front steps. Some kids came by on skateboards. They looked at me curiously but didn't speak. A wind came up, enough to whisk some candy wrappers down the pavement. I glanced up at the sky. Since the tornado, wind made me nervous. Some hero I was. What would I do if I had to live where there were tornadoes all the time? Or wars?

There were two kinds of heroes, I decided. There were the ones like me, who got a fuss made over them because they'd had the chance to help save some people. Then there was another kind of hero, like Aunt Henrietta. No one ever wrote stories in the newspapers about her. She was the kind of person who spent her whole life thinking about other people first. I think she is the best kind of hero.

After a time, Aunt Henrietta came out and sat down beside me. "Did you ever notice how it can seem like forever when you are waiting for something?" she said. "Then all of a sudden it's here and you wish you had more time."

I nodded. "Like Christmas. You wait and wait. Then it's the day before, and it makes you a little sad because you know in just a few hours it will be over."

"Exactly." Aunt Henrietta nodded.

She touched my arm. "I hope you won't be disappointed in me. I might not make it. There are some pretty rough hills in the last part of the race."

"I'll still be proud of you," I said. "Even if you don't make it all the way."

The next morning, Mrs. Sims drove us to Hopkinton. It was a really small town. We arrived at eight o'clock, and even though the race didn't begin until noon, the streets were packed. Aunt Henrietta pushed through the crowds. "I have to register and get my number," she said.

Aunt Henrietta was limping slightly when she came back. "I'm not sure you should try this with that ankle," Mom said.

"I've waited my whole life for this," Aunt Henrietta said. "I'm not giving up now." She pinned her number on her shirt. We watched as the runners started lining up. These were the champion runners who were competing to win the prizes. The ones with the fastest qualifying times were in the first rows. Aunt Henrietta was a long way back from them.

"Some of those runners will be done in a little over two hours," Aunt Henrietta said. "But they give out medals until five o'clock."

"We'll drive a few miles down the course," Mrs. Sims said. "Then we can cheer you on."

"Good luck, Aunt Henrietta," I said.

We stood on the sidelines for a few minutes, but with the growing crowd of runners, Aunt Henrietta was soon lost from view. "It will get better as it goes along," said Mrs. Sims. "A lot of people will drop out as the race goes on."

There were already hundreds of people lined up all along the route. We finally found a place to park near a town called Framingham and lined up to wait. There were people stationed along the way with water and other drinks for the runners as they raced past.

It was a cool day. "This is perfect weather for a race," Mom said.

"I think I'd like to do this someday," I said.

Mom looked surprised. "I know I'm not very athletic, but I really kind of enjoyed running with Aunt Henrietta," I explained.

"Here come the first runners," Mrs. Sims shouted. People cheered as the champion runners raced by. Row after row passed us. It didn't seem as if very many had dropped out of the race yet.

"Do you see Aunt Henrietta?" I asked as I tried to peer through the crowd.

"I see her," Mom shouted.

We waved as she ran by. Her face was scrunched up as though she was in pain, but she managed a smile for us as she passed.

Mrs. Sims jumped up and down with excitement. "Let's go up a little farther. Maybe we'll see her again."

We ran back to the car and looked for another spot. Traffic was heavy, and by the time we got back to the sidelines, the first runners had already passed. A man standing by me said that this was about the fifteen-mile mark. "The runners will make it to Newton Hills soon," he said. "There are four hills in about two miles. They call the last one Heartbreak Hill."

The runners were coming more slowly now, and they were farther apart. Instead of grabbing a drink on the run, some were stopping to rest.

"It's three o'clock," Mrs. Sims said. "The big runners are already done. She has to come pretty soon or she won't make it by five."

Almost as though she'd heard, Aunt Henrietta came into sight. I grabbed a cup of water and ran out to meet her. Aunt Henrietta looked terrible. Her face was pale, and she was running with a limp. "Maybe you should rest," I said.

She shook her head. "I don't think I could get started again," she said. She drank the water in big

161

gulps and handed back the cup as I ran a few paces beside her.

We climbed back in the car and headed for the finish line. The race ended in downtown Boston, and the traffic was so terrible that we didn't arrive until almost four-thirty. There was a place for family and friends to wait. Some of the crowd was already gone when we got there, but runners were still trickling in. Each one was given a medal. I glanced at Mom's watch. I could hardly stand the suspense. The minutes ticked on, closer and closer to the cutoff time.

Four-thirty passed and then four-forty-five. "She's not going to make it," I sighed. "All that work for nothing."

Mom put her arm around me and squeezed. "Aunt Henrietta did something she always wanted to do. So how could it be for nothing?"

Mrs. Sims looked at her watch. "She's only got five more minutes."

"Are you sure? Maybe your watch is fast," I said.

Mrs. Sims shook her head sympathetically.

I sat down on the side of the road.

"Wait, I see her!" Mom yelled. "I don't believe it. She's going to make it." Nearly a block down the road I saw Aunt Henrietta. She put on a little burst of speed as she saw us waving.

"Hurry!" I screamed. "It's almost time."

I saw her stumble and fall. "Oh no!" Mom cried.

The watching crowd moaned in sympathy. Aunt Henrietta struggled to her feet. Everyone cheered her on. "Come on, lady," someone called. "You can make it."

Aunt Henrietta's eyes were glued to the finish line. She seemed to make a superhuman effort as she crossed it. She jogged slowly to cool down as a woman put the medal around her neck.

"You made it, you made it!" I shouted.

Aunt Henrietta winked as she sagged against Mom and Mrs. Sims. "Of course I did," she said.

22

Home Again

WE STAYED ONLY one more day. Mom had a meeting with some engineers about the new highway on Wednesday afternoon, and she was worried that I would fall behind in school. Aunt Henrietta decided to stay a few days with Mrs. Sims to rest up before she headed to her new school. She promised to write as soon as she arrived.

Miss Lawson let me give a report about the race for extra credit. Even Steve and Lester, the biggest jocks in the room, seemed interested. "I'll bet I could do it," bragged Lester.

"Someday I really *am* going to run in the Boston Marathon," I told Willie and Marcia at lunch.

"I'll go with you," Willie said loyally.

I was glad to be back in my own bedroom, even though the house seemed empty without Aunt Henrietta. That night I took out the family tree Miss Lawson had given us back in January. Thanks to Aunt Henrietta I had most of the blanks filled in. I put a gold star next to Aunt Henrietta's name.

Dad noticed it on my desk when he came in to say good night. "A family is sort of like a tree," he said thoughtfully. "Like the leaves of a tree, we are all apart, and yet we are also connected."

"Aunt Henrietta gave us another family story, too," I said.

"Dad, can I flush?" Robbie called from the bathroom.

"No," we shouted together as we ran toward him.